DREADFUL DARK

Tales of Horror: Books 1 - 3

DEAN RASMUSSEN

Dreadful Dark
Tales of Horror: Book 1 - 3

Dean Rasmussen

For more information about this book, visit:

www.deanrasmussen.com
dean@deanrasmussen.com

Dreadful Dark: Tales of Horror: Books 1 - 3

Published by:

Dark Venture Press, 15502 Stoneybrook West Parkway, Suite 104-452, Winter Garden, FL 34787

Cover Art: Dark Venture Press and Deposit Photos

❀ Created with Vellum

More novels and stories coming soon!
Get a **FREE** short story!

https://books2read.com/StoneHill-BookOfCrane

www.deanrasmussen.com

BOOK 1

THE GARBAGE MAN

Those slimy rat bastards were at it again. Shovels clinked outside Skeeter's bedroom window.

He clutched at his hair and pulled. "I'll rip their heads off."

Soil and stones scraping against metal rose above the erratic whir of his air conditioner. He struggled out of bed and plodded over to the window. Moonlight lit his backyard and illuminated the outlines of two figures below. Pale ambience reflected off their rotted, gaunt faces. The male figure's black t-shirt and dark gray shorts camouflaged him within the darkness. The woman figure's blood-stained yellow dress stood out more clearly, and she swaggered as if drunk near the hole they were digging. Their sunken postures straightened when they saw him watching them.

They waved at him.

Arrogant bastards. He should have sawed their arms off when he had the chance. They were digging at an older gravesite, one that he had dug two years earlier.

It wasn't bad enough that the neighborhood kids rang his doorbell and ran away on a weekly basis, or stole his water hose, or strung toilet paper across the enormous oak tree in his front yard. But now even his nosy neighbors, Marcus Dipshit and his wife, Mrs. Supreme Leader Dipshit, regularly poked their wide-eyed, sun-browned faces over his fence to feed their insatiable curiosity regarding the nighttime antics in his backyard.

He needed over two hours of sleep. His head ached, and his vision shifted in and out of focus.

The woman in the yard below, Marlene had been her name, stood beside a mound of dirt at the edge of the unearthed grave and turned her smug face up at him. With a large, sweeping gesture she waved for him to come out and join them.

"You'd like that, wouldn't you? I'll pound your bones back to hell." Skeeter's breath fogged the window as he spoke.

Marlene's ratty hair shifted over her face as she swayed. It flowed over her cheeks and down to her shoulders. Even within the dim light, her grin beamed. The wench brushed her hair playfully and blew a kiss.

Skeeter's stomach churned. He'd take one of those shovels and lop her head off with it.

He slipped on a pair of pants, but left his upper half bare. The summer heat and the struggle to get the two back into their holes would have him sweating like a pig in no time. The digital clock next to his bed read 2:44.

He had struggled with them for over an hour the previous night and then filling the holes back in had pushed him to the brink of exhaustion. The damn arthritis in his hands and the pain in his back hadn't subsided after flaring up following the previous night's ordeal. Good thing it was Saturday or he would need to call in sick at work.

Skeeter lumbered down the stairs to the kitchen and crossed over to the garage door. The dirt from the previous night's ordeal still streaked across his floor. Another mess to clean up. Add it to the list.

On his way into the garage he remembered that his ax's handle had broken while struggling with a different set of the devil's demons. The large fat one had given him the most resistance. Skeeter had plowed the ax deep into the fat man's chest only to have the handle snap off when he yanked it back. Waste of a good thirty dollar ax. It had made little difference anyway, as the fat man continued the struggle without pausing. Skeeter had ended the problem by slicing off his head with a shovel.

A shotgun blast would do the trick in a heartbeat, but the neighbors would call the police in a heartbeat. Difficult to keep the evil insurrection down without a lot of noise. If it wasn't for his neighbors, he could blast away all he wanted. Problem solved.

Skeeter surveyed the inventory of his tools to consider the best plan of action. He had chains, shovels, a garden hoe, a rake, and a pile of bricks he'd intended to use to construct a more permanent disposal pit for the bodies. One shovel would do, as it had the previous night. Bits of rotted flesh still clung to the blade's edge.

Note to self: Clean that shit off.

Skeeter grabbed the shovel and stormed outside to the backyard.

The fence along his property's edge rose to eye level. It had been the highest fence he could find. Back then, he hadn't foreseen it being a problem.

The neighbor's bedroom light was on.

"Damn nosey neighbors," he grumbled.

He'd rip out that fence and build a new wall ten feet high. Made of brick. With spikes and barbed wire along the top edge.

Skeeter swung the shovel like a baseball bat as the male

figure came into focus ahead. The man's name had been Alan, one of the church members from across town. Skeeter had caught Alan and Marlene in the park fornicating. Skeeter had put an end to that shit. Never mind they were engaged. The park was only a hundred yards from the church. They might as well have been fornicating right in the holy sanctuary itself.

Alan stood waist deep within the hole he'd dug and continued scooping out shovelfuls of dirt even as Skeeter approached. The bastard had the same smart ass smug grin as the night he'd killed him. Skeeter's face warmed.

Marlene was a few feet away to the right, and she waved at Skeeter as if they were friends. Her jaw hung open as if to scream out in terror, but no sound came out of her throat. Skeeter wanted to chop her apart first, but Alan was closer and most likely stronger.

"You won't get to her," Skeeter said to them.

Alan and Marlene paid no attention.

Skeeter had buried the young woman, and everyone else, at least a few feet under. No chance of discovery—unless some asshole went digging in the right place. He'd long forgotten the woman's name. Tina? Tanya? What the hell did it matter? Skeeter's judgment had been just and righteous, and she had gotten what she deserved.

He was doing the town a favor. That's all there was to it. Cleaning up the trash and making the world a better place. Just disposing of all the disgusting filth in the community and doing the service for *free* at the same time. Nobody appreciated his work now, but they would in the future. They'd erect a statue to Skeeter in the center of town one day. Children would grow up praising his name for what he'd done for them.

The community was a better place now without filth like Marlene, Alan and... (Tracy?) creeping around the park at night and committing lewd acts in every corner like a sleazy brothel. The town could be made wholesome again. A family community with no room for immorality, just as it had been for him growing up, and he was chosen to uphold that morality, even if no one else was strong enough. Chosen by the family business he'd inherited.

He was the town's garbageman, after all. Just doing his job. All in a day's work. He'd taken care of the trash. Taken it out and buried it.

But now it came back.

Skeeter rotated his shovel so the blade would slice across when he swung. He was too furious to bother creeping up on them, and besides Marlene had already seen him. He timed it so that Alan's shovel was down in the hole before he swung. Skeeter grunted as he swung, aiming toward the neck.

Alan's shovel shot up from the hole at the last second. Metal clinked and a jolt of vibration raced up Skeeter's arms. Alan had not only stopped his own decapitation, but Skeeter's shovel flew from his sweaty palms and spun off to the opposite side of the grave.

Skeeter ground his teeth. "You piece of shit."

He drew back for a moment, and then a raging fury flooded his mind. He charged forward and dropped to his knees, clutching Alan around the neck. Skeeter would pop Alan's skull from his spine like popping the head from a dandelion with his thumb.

Alan dropped his shovel and grabbed onto Skeeter's wrists. Alan's leathery rotting flesh scratched across Skeeter's skin and he winced as Alan clamped down harder.

Skeeter sneered and dug his thumbs into Alan's throat. The windpipe collapsed. He pushed harder, straight through the icy strands of rotted muscles to Alan's spinal cord. A few more seconds and it'd be over.

"Hold still," Skeeter said. "Almost finished with you."

One vertebra cracked. Skeeter strained and shook within

his rage. Sweat dripped down his forehead. His left hand pulled Alan's neck down and his right hand stretched it up. One of Alan's neck muscles tore and snapped apart. Then another.

A metal object smashed against the side of Skeeter's head. A flash of light as pain exploded in his skull. He toppled over and wobbled at the edge of the grave.

Marlene's shovel rose again and came down hard against his thigh. Pain surged up his spine. Skeeter twisted himself around and the shovel slammed down against the back of his right calf. He didn't stop, and within his daze Marlene grabbed at his legs. She yanked him closer to the grave, but he threw up his aching leg and kicked into the darkness. The sole of his boot slammed into her chest, and she tumbled backwards beyond his sight.

Skeeter grabbed at the clumps of grass and dirt that surrounded him and gasped for breath as he turned himself over and rolled onto his chest. His pulse pounded in his ears as he staggered to his feet. Before he could take his first step a hand clutched at his ankle and he almost fell forward onto his face again. He looked back. Alan was using Skeeter's ankle to tow himself out of the hole.

Skeeter's boot loosened as he struggled to get away. He looked around for anything he might use as a weapon. Nothing.

"Son of a bitch." Skeeter thrashed his foot until he knocked Alan away and scrambled to stand again.

There had to be something in his garage to deal with the problem. Something better than a shovel. Something to send them back to hell once and for all. But without resorting to a shotgun, he didn't have many options. He took in a lungful of air and hurried back to the house.

On his way in through the garage, he grabbed the last shovel and brought it with him into the kitchen in case he needed it. In the morning he'd run to the store and purchase a shitload of axes to chop up those yard bastards. Or maybe something better.

A wood chipper. He'd buy one tomorrow. Why hadn't he thought of it sooner? That'd put the uprising to a rest. The idea perked up his mind, but his body slouched forward. The stores wouldn't open for several more hours.

He flipped on the kitchen light and his eyes narrowed as he searched the counters for any large knives. He found one butcher's knife in a drawer and grabbed it. Next, he walked to his kitchen pantry and dug out two pistols, a rifle, and a shotgun, and scooped up a handful of rounds. He gathered everything, shovel and all, and carried the weapons to his bedroom upstairs.

He dropped everything at the end of his bed. Something clanked outside, and he hurried to the window. Alan and Marlene had continued digging within the grave they had started earlier. Marlene looked up at him, but this time she didn't wave. This time she pointed down into the open grave.

"I'll chop you up into little bite-size pieces," Skeeter said. "That wood chipper will do the trick. And after that's done, I'll dump a few bags of wet cement over you. Squirm your slimy way out of that."

Skeeter went to load his guns just in case he needed to use them, but only as a last resort. One shot and his neighbors wouldn't hesitate to call the cops. A few minutes later he'd have a bigger problem on his hands with the current state of his backyard. It'd be all over. He wouldn't have the time or the strength to fill in the graves before they arrived. Guns were the nuclear option.

He had a right to defend himself against attackers, especially demonic attackers from the bowels of hell, but he doubted a judge would express sympathy in his case.

"We counted seventeen bodies in your backyard, Mr. Larsten," the judge would say. "How do you explain that?"

"I didn't know they were there, Your Honor."

"Some of them were freshly dug. You weren't aware of anyone burying corpses in your fenced backyard?"

"No, Your Honor, honestly. I never saw a thing."

"Some of them were riddled with bullet holes matching guns found in your home. How do you explain that?"

"Circumstantial evidence, Your Honor."

Not good.

As he finished loading his last gun, someone pounded on the back door downstairs. He stopped for a moment and listened. They couldn't get in—except for the garage door. All the entrances and windows were well boarded up with large sheets of plywood to seal himself in. If he wanted to see sunlight, he'd go upstairs and look out his bedroom window.

He'd boarded everything up a few days ago, after seeing the undead digging around in his backyard at night. At first the figures had only stood next to their holes after digging themselves out, and for him to kick them back into their graves had been easy, but now somehow they had found shovels and had dug out the others. The previous night three of them had climbed out and stood watching his bedroom window, swaying in the cool spring breeze.

"Go back to hell!" He yelled from behind the glass. He wanted to scream it from the open window, except for the neighbors. They were past the point of tolerance with him and were itching to make that last call that would send a swarm of officers to investigate his property.

The phone rang. The Caller ID read 'Unknown Number' and he hesitated to answer it. It rang again. He picked it up. Probably his neighbor to complain about the noise.

"What?" he grumbled.

A woman's voice gurgled and croaked back at him. He

remembered her name now. It was Twyla. She had made the same noises years earlier when he had wrung the life out of her in the park. Skeeter had caught her one night with a man who was not her husband. The garbage man would take that trash out of town. Bury it a little closer to its home in hell.

"Into the fires of hell, Twyla! Meet your judgment!" He ended the phone call, but it continued to ring over and over. He powered it off, stopping it in mid-ring. He wiped the sweat from his brow and went to the thermostat in the hallway to crank up the air conditioning.

Despite the figures staring at him, he snapped the blinds shut and collapsed onto his bed, gripping his shotgun over his chest. The lack of sleep was catching up to him. His eyes dropped shut and his mind wandered even as the work of the devil's angels continued in his backyard. If they were still there in the morning, he'd deal with it then. He closed his eyes.

SKEETER FADED BACK TO CONSCIOUSNESS AS SOMETHING thumped against the side of the house. According to the clock next to his bed, only forty-three minutes had passed. Skeeter trudged over to the window again and opened the blind. Impossible to think they could climb up the sides of the house to the second floor. But since the bastards had discovered shovels, maybe they would also find the ladder in his garage. Had they broken in there? He strained to see anything near the house below his line of sight. Only darkness.

Alan and Marlene were still at it. Alan flung the dirt to the side as the trench below him deepened. It wouldn't take him long now to reach the corpse within it.

Skeeter regretted not burying them all deeper.

Note to self: Pour cement in the holes next time before covering them over.

Hell, he'd pound a wooden stake through their damned hearts, sever their heads, and shove a dozen crucifixes down their throats if he got the chance to do it over, and then he'd still pour a foot of cement on top for good measure.

He'd survived two tours in the Vietnam war, attacked by some of the most savage and skilled fighters in the Viet Cong's army, and he'd survived their worst. The last mortar attack had blown through his left knee, shortening that leg by two full inches after the doctors had patched him back together. He'd seen hell, an actual hell, and was ready for those demons outside his house like a tank was ready to battle monkeys with sticks.

Alan stared up at Skeeter's bedroom window as he stood chest deep in the hole. His mouth gaped open as if to call out.

Skeeter raised his middle finger at them before snapping the blinds shut. He returned to bed listening to Alan's shovel slicing into the soil followed by a thud of dirt dropping next to the grave.

They couldn't get at him, but he didn't take any chances. The weapons he'd carried upstairs would be enough in case the worst happened. On top of that, he stocked his basement with plenty of dried food and water, in case of emergencies.

He closed his eyes in bed until the shoveling ended.

Everything became silent. A ringing in his ears intensified for several minutes before he got up and shuffled to the window. Alan and Marlene were gone, and the gravesites sat wide open. Three in all now.

The doorbell rang and Skeeter shuddered. He clenched his teeth and squeezed the barrel of the shotgun as he lurched toward the door, grabbing the shovel with his other hand. The shovel wasn't the most effective weapon, but it worked well enough for now if he wanted to keep things quiet. He charged downstairs, dropped the shovel to the ground, and stood behind the front door with the barrel of the shotgun aimed waist high at whoever stood on the other side.

The doorbell rang again. Someone pounded on the door. "Skeeter!"

It was the muffled voice of Mr. Dipshit himself.

"What the hell are you doing? It's 4 AM."

Skeeter lowered the shotgun. "Get the hell off my property!"

"I'll have the cops out here if you don't quiet down," King Marcus Dipshit yelled. "What the hell are you doing in the backyard?"

"None of your goddamn business."

"I'll have the cops out here."

The neighbor's footsteps squeaked away across the porch. A moment later someone pounded on the back door. Marcus couldn't have gotten around to the back that fast. And the gate was locked. Alan and Marlene, no doubt.

Skeeter lifted his shotgun again and rushed to the back of the house with wide eyes. He left the lights off, although a hallway light from upstairs spilled down the stairway. He approached the back door with the shotgun held up at chest level.

Something crashed in his basement. He'd boarded up those windows too, although not as well as the larger main floor windows. If they'd somehow gotten in the basement, he was ready for them.

He might have to weed them out of his house like cockroaches. Maybe that was better, anyway. Less commotion to attract the ire of his neighbors.

If he could trap them all in one room, he had a better chance of handling the mess at the same time. The basement would be the best place. Lots of room down there to defend himself and lots of light. In addition, his neighbors might not hear the shotgun blasts over at their house, since the only window to the basement faced away from them. That might be the way to go. The more he thought about it, the more he liked it.

He approached the back door and watched the door handle turn as he steadied the shotgun. If he fired through the door, he might miss and one shot alone might prompt his neighbor to live up to his threat of calling the police.

Something thumped against the door. The walls creaked.

"I know your game," Skeeter said. They were trying to distract him at the back door while someone came in through the basement.

He hurried back over to the front door, picked up the shovel where he'd left it, then headed for the basement. The head of the shovel clanked against the edge of the doorway going down to the basement. He flipped on the light and expected one of them to be waiting for him at the bottom of the stairs, but he was alone. Each footstep creaked as he descended with the shotgun up and ready.

"Yeah, we'll solve this problem right now."

He crept all the way to the bottom of the stairs when the lights cut out. His heart raced and in the darkness something scraped across the tiled floor.

A hoarse gurgling filled the air. Twyla was down there with him. The sounds shifted closer, but he couldn't tell from where.

He stumbled backwards and raced up the stairs.

At the top step he paused and set down the shovel, leaning it against the wall. He fumbled for the emergency flashlight he kept hanging on a nail above the light switch. He gasped for breath when he found it and switched it on.

Twyla was at the bottom of the stairs, staring up at him

with sunken, bug-infested eyes. She drifted and straightened her back. Dirt matted her hair against her face and rotting flesh scraped along the railing as she stepped up the stairs toward him.

Her purple and white dress brought back memories of the night he'd killed her. Her cries for mercy on that Judgment Day. He showed no mercy. No room for mercy in the garbage man's judgement.

"Judge... you," Twyla said in a wet, gurgled tone.

"I'm blameless, honey," Skeeter blurted out. "You're the skank who cheated on your husband."

Twyla had been a young woman from his church. The night he killed her and her partner in the affair, his rage had swelled inside his chest. He'd swung at them like the god Thor, striking each of them down with only one blow. He'd laughed while burying them with their lungs still gasping for breath. Strange that Twyla stood there alone. Skeeter scanned the room for her partner, but they were alone. Alan and Marlene must not have had time to dig out Twyla's fornicating friend.

Twyla took another step toward him. Skeeter set his shotgun down and picked up his shovel. She was a scrawny, short woman and he would send her back to hell. No need to make more noise than necessary. The shovel would do nicely.

He moved back down the stairs and lifted the shovel like a spear, holding the flashlight in the other hand. One straight crack to the head should do it.

The basement window caught his eye for a moment before he struck Twyla. He missed his target, and the shovel grazed off the edge of her skull.

He stopped himself within an arm's length of her. The putrid smell of decaying flesh wafted into his face. She reached out at him as he glanced over to the basement window. Someone had pulled away the sheet of plywood he had used to seal the window shut on one side and a man was crawling in—Twyla's fornicating partner.

The man's corpse plummeted and slammed onto a workbench below the window, crashing into an assortment of tools and failed home improvement projects. Skeeter had never discovered the name of Twyla's affair partner. The man squirmed and climbed off the workbench and stood unsteadily before them.

Skeeter raised his shovel again, but before he could slice it through Twyla's neck, she batted it away and wrapped her fingers around his neck. She pushed forward, and he stopped breathing.

Twyla's partner rushed toward them, but Skeeter twisted around and broke free from Twyla's grasp.

He heaved in a deep breath and knocked away their hands. "You think I'm playing? You think this is a game?"

He stomped up the stairs to get his shotgun. No more playing around. He would get the job done.

Halfway up the stairs his foot slipped and his knee slammed against the edge of a step.

"Shit!" he yelled.

He stumbled and grabbed the railing as footsteps stomped up behind him.

One of them gripped his pant leg and pulled.

Skeeter jabbed the end of the shovel backwards, knocking into one of them. A low growl erupted from the man's throat as Skeeter moved freely until they latched onto the shovel handle. They ripped it away from him, but it didn't matter, anyway. He was only feet from the shotgun. He lunged forward and grabbed it.

Skeeter spun around with the shotgun in his hand and blasted off three shots in rapid succession. Hell with the neighbors.

He fumbled with the flashlight during the blasts,

witnessing the upper half of their bodies explode. The first two shots disintegrated the man and the third one took down Twyla. Their mangled corpses tumbled back down the stairs.

Skeeter's ears rang. "Evil, evil, evil." He fired a fourth shot at them, but his shotgun clicked empty. All his ammo was up in his bedroom.

He lumbered up the stairs into the kitchen. The back door was still sealed shut. The eerie quiet of his house without power sank in on him. He shined the flashlight at each window. No sign of forced entry.

He trudged upstairs, his body weakening with each step. His legs were on fire by the time he got to the top. He caught his breath and steadied himself against the wall.

"The garbage man's got a job to do," he said, trudging into his bedroom.

He took inventory of the remaining firearms and boxes of rounds on his bed.

Something thumped against the wall below his bedroom window.

"Son of a bitch."

Skeeter's head ached as he squinted toward the closed blinds. The bastards couldn't climb the side of his house, so what the hell was out there?

He plodded to the window again, opened the blinds and Marlene's gaunt face met his eyes. She smashed her arm in through the glass, with shards spraying over his face and bare chest. Blood dripped down his face within seconds and he stumbled backwards.

Before he could defend himself, her torso folded in over the top of the windowsill. He retrieved his revolver from the edge of the bed and fired at her, knowing full well that Mr. Dipshit would either call the police or come stomping over to his front door in minutes. The rounds passed through her face and neck. Black ooze drained from the holes.

"Evil woman," he shouted.

She clawed at him without hesitation. "My turn," she said in a low, growling voice.

"Get back in your hole!" He fired the revolver's remaining rounds until it emptied and dropped it to the floor. He grabbed a metal trophy next to his window he'd received as a child for demonstrating exemplary Christian behavior in Sunday school and slammed it into Marlene's face.

It cracked into her skull, collapsing it, leaving one eye and her nose distorted sideways. More black ooze erupted from her nose and mouth and ran down her dress. Some of it splattered over his face and pooled on his forehead. It dripped down between his eyebrows. He wiped it away with the back of his wrist, which only smeared it into his eyes.

Alan appeared beside Marlene and each of them clutched one of Skeeter's arms. Heaving together, they dragged him toward the window. He struggled, but he was too exhausted to resist. He writhed and weakened until they yanked him head-first out into the chilly morning air.

Glass shards along the edges of the window sliced through his body on the way out. The pain shot through him like a blow torch, lit up against his ribcage and spread up across the side of his face. Warm blood soaked down his pants as they lowered him along the side of the house by his feet, his arms flailing below. They didn't let him drop to the ground where he would certainly have broken his neck.

When his fingers touched the ground he clawed at the grass. More hands waited to clutch onto him from below. He recognized some of them in the moonlight. All of them faces of filthy, evil garbage.

"You are all disgusting," he shrieked.

As they dragged him toward one of the open pits, more figures joined the growing crowd around him, and they spun him around so he faced them. They stretched his limbs in all directions over one of the graves.

In one final coordinated effort they released him face up into the pit. He crashed to the bottom. Loose dirt splashed down onto his face, slipping into his nose and his mouth. The chunks of soil and stones pounded against his chest as he struggled to stand up. His lower body sank below the dirt and then his chest. His fingers clawed against the walls of the pit, scratching through worms and plant roots.

A red and orange flashing light gradually lit up the figures above him. Skeeter's eyes widened, and he grinned. His nosy neighbor had finally called the police.

He laughed. "They'll be here in minutes! You're too late. I win!"

His chest filled with exhilaration, knowing that the garbage towering over him would never have their victory.

The dirt piled in. It was up to his chin within a minute, but he only laughed louder.

"Only one way to get rid of garbage," Marlene gurgled. "The incinerator."

He laughed until the heat rose up from below. The orange and red lights from above mirrored the flickering flames from below. His feet and legs burned. The pain grew more intense and spread up his body.

Claws scratched up and down his backside. Rats? His heart pounded as one claw dug into the center of his back and clutched his spine.

His captors dragged him further into the pit. He sank, drowning in the incinerator until it consumed him.

THE ONE

Which you be so kind as to watch my jacket while I play a game of pool with these young ladies?"

We were hoping to meet a few fun-loving honeys at the bar, but we met David instead. He was dressed up like a modern-day mobster—something you'd see on one of those TV shows for cops—with slicked-back hair and a stoic gaze that chilled your blood. A fancy black leather jacket covered a gray shirt with some top-of-the-line jeans to catch a girl's eye. The guy had all the looks we would have killed for.

He was there when we arrived, slipping in between two hotties like a knife through butter. One was a blonde chick with a short black skirt and a tight white t-shirt that revealed a piercing in her navel. The other girl had tanned skin and long brown hair pulled together in the back. She wore tight jeans and a red low-cropped shirt that revealed a little cleavage. Neither of the girls seemed to mind as David caressed them openly.

Only ten minutes after we arrived, he swaggered over to us, extending his leather jacket to no one in particular. "Would you be so kind as to watch my jacket while I play a game of pool with these young ladies?"

We all stared at the jacket like it was covered in dog shit. It tempted me to tell him to go fuck himself. Did I look like a coat closet? But he caught me off-guard. Something about his eyes stunned me, and those two chicks were eyeing me up too.

"Yeah." I accepted his jacket and hung it off the back of my barstool.

David strolled back over to his business at the pool table.

"The hell with that guy." Butch glanced at the jacket. "Check the pockets."

Luis laughed and sipped his beer.

I shot a glance toward the pool table. David wasn't paying any attention to us. "You want to get killed? That guy's got to be packing heat."

"Pussy," Butch said.

I expected Butch or Luis to dig into the jacket's pockets, but they left it alone too.

Butch made a crude gesture while detailing his fantasized intentions for the girls after getting them into his bed later that evening. Not a chance in hell that would happen. Butch smelled like he hadn't taken a shower in a week. In reality, it was probably more like two.

Within seconds of returning to the pool table, David was showing the two girls how to play the game. We had nothing better to do, so we hung around and watched the master hit on the girls. It was a work of art, actually, the way David ran his fingers along their shoulders and arms as they lined up the pool cue. They soaked it all up, every slick move he dished out to them. A lot of gentle touches with only a quick glance every so often. Most of the time he ignored them. Within minutes they nuzzled up next to him, both of them almost fighting to be the center of his attention.

He sure had the right attitude, and a smile loaded with bright white teeth. Something straight off the cover of a GQ magazine. He strutted around the table before every shot, I guess to see which chick could catch up to him the fastest. After each perfect shot he stood up straight, leaning against the pool cue, with a tall, confident posture.

He shot us a devious grin every once in a while as he worked his magic on the girls. He had to know we were staring. How could we *not* stare? After a while he even maneuvered one girl around, leaning her over the table's edge during one shot so her ass stuck out in our direction. God bless him. Didn't block our view or anything. He must have figured we were losers and wanted to share in the spoils of his conquest. Fine with us. Much appreciated.

We'd gotten there late, so before long the bartender yelled it was closing time and flipped on the lights. The harsh glare blinded me for a moment, but soon enough the reality of our situation hit me. Three losers going home alone again without girls.

David threw his arms around the girls and looked over at us. The girls cuddled up at his sides.

I finished my drink and tried to stand tall, but we couldn't hide our situation. We were going home empty-handed.

None of this shit would have happened if we'd just taken off then. But Butch locked his gaze on the blonde girl and insisted on waiting until she left.

The tanned girl locked eyes with me and smiled. My heart melted. I just about fell off that bar stool—no joke. She walked over to me and I lost my breath as she reached her hand around my back. She smelled like a dozen roses.

"Excuse me." She moved in a little closer. "I need to get his jacket." She tugged on David's jacket.

"Sorry." I leaned forward to free it from my stool.

"What's your name?" she asked.

"Jacob."

"I'm Emily. You up for a party? We're heading out now."

David cozied up to the blonde girl near the pool table. Emily leaned in, rubbing her thigh against my knee.

She was way out of my league, and the last thing I needed was that gangster dude beating me down for messing with his girl. "Maybe some other time."

Emily pouted. "Aw, you don't like me?" Her green eyes never looked away.

"You're beautiful, but—" I glanced back to David.

She laughed. "Don't mind him. I'm not his girlfriend."

I glanced over to Butch and Luis. They nodded with wide eyes.

Emily stroked her fingers across my cheek, pulling my attention back to her. "We should get to know each other. You're cute."

David strolled over a moment later and claimed his jacket from Emily. Instead of putting it on, he swept it over his shoulder. The blonde girl nuzzled up to him. "Thanks for watching my jacket," he said. "You boys up for a party? My name's David."

Butch shrugged without smiling. "Maybe."

David grinned at me. "I see you've met Emily. Don't worry, she's not attached to me." He gestured to the blonde girl. "This is Zoey. She's unattached as well."

"Cool," Butch said.

He shook our hands. Tight grip. I winced until he let go, and he smirked as if he got a kick out of my reaction. That guy's grasp could have ripped my arm off if he sneezed.

"We're heading to my girlfriend's place," David said. "You'll all get laid. Guaranteed."

Emily elbowed David in his side, her gaze still locked on me.

Butch scanned Zoey's dress. Luis glanced at me.

The blonde girl whispered into David's ear, pulling him down toward her. The edge of his shirt stretched open to reveal a tattoo on his neck, a design that reminded me of the devil. A serpentine red arm snaked up from the collar of his shirt, holding a pitchfork capped with three sharp prongs. A single word stretched out below the image, but I didn't get close enough to read it.

"How far?" I asked.

"Not far," David said. "Ten, fifteen minutes."

"You got beer?" Butch asked.

"We've got everything," David said. "Follow me."

We followed David to the exit. Emily walked beside me in silence all the way to our car before we split off to our separate cars.

"See you there, Jacob." Emily glanced back as she walked away.

Butch and Luis ordered me to drive, probably because they thought I wasn't as drunk as they were. We climbed into our rusting hulk of a car and followed David's white Lexus.

Emily and Zoey climbed into a red Toyota RAV4 and took off in a different direction.

"Where the fuck are they going?" Butch said from the back seat. "Follow them!"

I looked at Luis. He pointed toward David's car.

"Follow the dude," Luis said. "Maybe they're stopping to pick up their friends. Two babes aren't enough to go around, anyway."

"See you later, Jacob," Luis mocked.

"You're jealous," I said.

"Damn right."

"You see Zoey looking at me?" Butch asked. "She wants me."

"Dude, she was looking at *me*, not you."

"Jacob, back me up here. You saw her staring at me, right?"

"I wasn't paying attention."

"Right. That Emily chick was hot for you. Lucky man."

Luis held his palm up for a high five. I slapped it.

"She's The One, Jacob." Luis nodded. "I can tell. You guys had chemistry."

"We'll see." I focused on the road.

We headed around through the winding city streets until turning into a dark residential area a few miles from the bar. Nothing special about the neighborhood. Not the mansions we'd expected from David's appearance, but not a slum either. Just your ordinary suburban row of working-class homes.

As we turned down one long stretch of houses, Luis reached down to the floor between his feet and pulled up a baseball bat. He brought his bat everywhere.

"Slow down." He gestured to a mailbox at the side of the road. The little red flag at the side of the box was up. "There."

I knew what to do. I slowed the car down and came up alongside it. Luis leaned out and swung. The bat cracked against the metal mailbox and the little door flew open, spewing letters of blood.

"Bullseye!" Luis yelled as he sat back in his seat.

"Ready for the big leagues!" Butch patted him on the shoulder.

"I've trained for this all my life."

With the windows down and the stereo pumping out rock tunes, we turned onto a barren street and into an area of the city I didn't recognize.

"He better not bring us to some shit hole," Butch said. "We can hang out at Luis's apartment for that."

"Fuck off. Don't come over anymore if you don't like it."

"You never bring home any girls."

"Says Mr. Casanova, alone in the backseat."

As we drove further, the quality of the houses improved. Maybe it wouldn't be so bad after all. I couldn't read the street names since I guess I'd had one too many at the bar. At that point, it didn't even matter where we were because my mind floated back to Emily.

"What the hell's this dude's name again?" Luis asked. "Dan?"

For a moment I forgot the guy's name, then I remembered. "David."

"Better be some hot chicks," he said.

"And beer," Butch said.

"You'll get laid tonight for sure," Luis said to Butch in the backseat. "I can't believe you're twenty-one and still a virgin."

"It won't be a problem," he answered. "I'll make her scream."

"She'll scream, all right, as she runs away!"

"Fuck you."

David pulled his car over a few blocks down the road. I pulled up behind him. The walkways and streets around those houses in that neighborhood were well lit. A massive rock waterfall sat behind the beaming sign out front. Terrace Gardens Homes. Decked out landscaping everywhere, with a row of red and white flowers bordering the property. If that swanky neighborhood was any sign of the quality of the girls who lived there, we were in for one hell of a good night.

We all climbed out and stood beside the car, waiting for David to come over. He sat there in the driver's seat for a few minutes with the lights on. Making some calls, no doubt, to round up more hotties. He emerged wearing sunglasses. How the hell he saw anything with those sunglasses on in the dark, I have no idea.

"You boys are in for a treat," David said. "This will be a night to remember." He lit a cigarette and dangled it from his lips as he swaggered past us toward the front steps.

David paused at the front door as he flipped through the

keys on his key chain. The first key didn't work. Or the second key. Or the third.

"Damn, it's here somewhere," David said. He tried to open the door without a key and it creaked open. He chuckled as he slipped his keys back into his jacket pocket. "Forgot to lock it."

David opened the door slowly, peeking through the crack for a moment before walking in.

"Hey there," he called out, glancing around the house without flipping on the lights. "You home, sweetheart?"

An overwhelming smell of roses filled the air. David flipped on the lights. No flowers anywhere. Must have been scented candles or something.

Paintings of flowers and risque portraits of an attractive red-haired woman hung on the walls. The living room furniture looked clean and new and perfectly coordinated colors filled the room. It looked like one of those model showrooms in a furniture store. They lined the mantel over the fireplace with crystal vases, and everything looked as if they'd designed it to fit in that exact space. Everything was super clean and nothing was out of place, except for our three sorry asses.

David turned to us. "You guys just hang out here," he said. "I'll be back in a minute with the girls. This is my girlfriend's place. Stay out of the bedrooms, though. Don't go snooping. Cool? Hang tight. Chill. Watch some TV. There are beers in the fridge, but I'll get more. Don't you worry."

David slipped past us out the door and he was gone. We stood there looking at each other for an awkward moment until Butch hurried over to the fridge. Luis dropped into the living room couch and turned on the TV.

"Fuck yeah!" Butch said from the kitchen. He held up a bottle of vodka. "No shortage of booze." He poured some in three glasses, mixed it with some orange juice and handed one to me. "He said to chill, so chill."

Butch carried the other two glasses over to the living room and collapsed next to Luis. I sat on a different section of the couch. Luis flipped through the TV channels, stopping on one of those adult channels that only teased the viewers.

WITHIN HALF AN HOUR BUTCH AND LUIS HAD FINISHED their vodka drinks and several beers. I grabbed the last beer and claimed my space in front of the TV, which the others had abandoned.

Luis stared out the living room window toward the street. "What the fuck is taking him so long?"

The portraits of the redhead around the room fixated Butch as if he was in a trance. "Look at those tits. Just perfect."

I went over to get a better look. The girl in the pictures was beautiful, as if a professional had taken the portraits. A model? Just the type of girl who'd fawn over a slick stud like David. Maybe the man himself had taken the photos.

"Very nice." I stepped sideways to view every one of them.

"Nice?" Butch focused on one photo of the girl in a bikini. "She's hot. Beyond hot. She's gorgeous. I'd lay my face right in there and..." Butch shook his head, while making growling sounds.

"Maybe you'll get your chance," I said.

Butch stared at me and wavered with a wide grin on his face. "That David guy better get his ass back here. I'm ready to party *now*!"

Butch staggered away while I checked out the other pictures around the room. He went down the hall and started opening all the doors. I assumed he was looking for the bathroom.

"Hey, dumb shit," I said, "the dude told you to stay out of the bedrooms."

"Fuck that," Butch said. "I'm going to snoop through his shit. Serves him right for leaving us here alone for almost an hour."

"Definitely a chick's pad." Luis munched on a bag of snack chips in the kitchen. "No guy would ever keep it this clean."

Butch opened the last door at the end of the hallway and his mouth dropped open. "What the fuck?"

"What is it?" Luis asked.

"Get the fuck over here!"

Luis and I hurried over to see what Butch was staring at. I rolled my eyes on the way over, thinking Butch was setting us up for a massive prank. He was a dick like that, so when I got to his side and looked into the room I braced myself for his wild laughter.

But he wasn't joking. My mouth dropped open too. A naked girl was lying on the bed with her hands and feet tied with duct tape to the headboard and footboard. Her mouth was also duct-taped shut and her hair was a mess. The same red-haired girl from the portraits over the walls. Some sheets lay in a heap on the floor, surrounded by stuff you might find on a nightstand. The clock and lamp were smashed as if someone had thrown them there. The girl's eyes were closed, and she wasn't moving at all.

"What the fuck is going on here?" Luis asked.

"Is she dead?" Butch leaned forward.

Her chest rose and fell in shallow waves. "She's breathing."

"Let's get the fuck out of here," I said.

Butch crept toward the girl. "Hey."

No response.

He spoke louder. "Hey!" He reached out and touched the girl's leg.

"Come on," I said. "She must be passed out. Let's go."

"Hold on," Butch said. "Look at those glorious tits." He reached out and touched the girl's breasts.

"Dude, I don't want anything to do with this," I said.

"You want a feel?" he asked us. He cupped his hands around the bottom and squeezed.

"No, Butch," Luis said. "Stop. I think someone raped her. Maybe that David guy."

Butch stopped and gazed at her face.

The girl's eyes opened wide. She stared at Butch, then over to Luis, then at me. Her eyes opened wider as she let out a muffled scream beneath the tape over her mouth. Her eyes were bloodshot, and she squirmed, kicking and pulling against the restraints on her limbs. The tape covering her mouth slid back and forth as she contorted her face to remove it. The whole bed shook just like one of those demon possession scenes in The Exorcist. Butch stumbled backwards.

"We got to go." I nudged Luis toward the door.

Butch stared at her and folded his arms over his chest. "Stop wiggling around."

Luis rushed forward and pulled on Butch's shirt. "Come on."

Butch twisted away and continued to stare. "You don't see stuff like this every day, Luis. Isn't she beautiful? Jacob, get your ass over here."

"No way," I said. "Let's just go now."

Luis pulled on Butch's arm again and this time got Butch out of the room. We left the door wide open and headed for the front door.

"Wait." Luis stopped me as I opened the door. "Fuckin' stop."

"What?" I asked, still holding the door handle.

Luis stepped forward and shut the door. "Listen. I have a bad feeling about all this. Someone obviously raped her. I think this is a setup. That David fucking guy isn't coming back. I can see that now. And thanks to doofus here," Luis gestured to Butch, "she not only saw our faces, but she knows our names. That David guy knew we'd go snooping, and he knew we'd find her. It's a setup."

"We didn't do that shit to her," Butch said.

"I know that, but she woke up with you groping her, dumbass. What is she going to think? That David guy must have drugged her and set us up."

"Fuck, Butch," I said, running my fingers through my hair, "why did you go in there?"

"I was just looking around," Butch said. "It's not my fault. *I* didn't fucking rape her."

"Well," Luis said, "she stared right at each of us. She can ID us. Guaranteed."

"Butch, you're a fucking idiot," I said.

Butch grabbed the front of my shirt and clenched his teeth, pushing me back into the door. "Shut the fuck up."

His eyes and face were red, and I turned my head away to avoid breathing in the warm stench of his beer breath.

Butch shoved me again. "You're the asshole who started talking to that David piece of shit loser. *You* got us into this mess."

"What the hell, guys," Luis said, staring at the floor, folding his hands on top of his head. "What are we going to do?"

Butch pushed me aside, went to the kitchen and started opening drawers.

I found the door handle behind me again. "Let's just go."

"Nobody's going anywhere," Butch said. "I know what to do."

"What are you talking about?" Luis asked.

I opened the door, and Butch came over grasping a large butcher's knife.

"Where are you going?" He slammed the door closed again.

He grabbed my shirt with his free hand and launched me across the floor. My right arm cracked down first, and a sharp pain shot through my back. I caught my breath. Butch loomed over me, brandishing the knife.

"Don't even think of running out on us, you little pussy." Butch slammed his foot down on my chest. He pinned me to the floor for a moment while I gasped for air. "Should I tie you up like that girl?"

I shook my head. "Damn, chill out."

"I'll solve this problem. Got it? I'm not going to prison over this shit."

"Wait," Luis said, "what are you planning to do?"

"Solve the problem." Butch swung the knife in Luis's face.

"You can't kill her."

"Why not? She can ID us now." Butch heaved in and out with each breath.

"Let's think about this."

"You got a better idea?"

"No," Luis said.

"Dead men tell no tales," Butch said, lifting his foot off my chest. "Or dead women."

Butch walked down the hall toward the girl in the bedroom.

I struggled to stand and Luis helped me to my feet. "We got to stop him."

Luis bit his nails. "I got a friend I can call. Come in here and wipe the place clean."

"Dude, we're not murderers. Butch is out of control."

"*I'm* not murdering anyone." Luis was hunched forward, still biting his nails. "I guess it's the only way to get us out of this. He's covering our asses. What choice do we have?"

I put my hand on the cellphone in my pocket. "We can call 911."

Luis looked at me as if I'd suggested we French kiss. "Are you nuts? You don't seem to understand the situation we're in. Butch is right. This is *your* fault for schmoozing with some low-life asshole. I knew right away the guy was a dick."

I scanned the house, as if something miraculous would present a way out of the mess. The TV blared, showing a bunch of lifeguards scrambling into the ocean to save someone from drowning. A gorgeous redhead cried on the shore, comforted by some macho dude.

If I could only get Butch to wait until we came up with a better plan. But Butch never wasted time. He always ran with the first thing that popped into his mind. That attitude was loads of fun in a party setting, but now the party was over. I never wanted to drink another beer in my life. My heart thumped in my ears as everything around me became crystal clear.

I wanted to do something. The image of the girl in the bedroom squirming in terror at seeing us played over and over in my mind. Her muffled cries streamed through the hallway, and chills passed through my chest. I crossed my arms over my chest to keep my hands from shaking.

"We shouldn't do this," I said.

Luis slammed his fist into my arm. "Butch is right. You are a pussy." He crossed around in front of me and got in my face. "Are you going to keep your mouth shut?" Luis shivered and sneered.

"Butch doesn't have to kill her," I said. "There's got to be a better way."

"Not a peep from you." Luis dug his index finger into my chest. "Not another word. We won't ever talk about this again."

Butch was in the bedroom for a long time. Luis glanced at

a large clock on the wall every few seconds. The TV show with the lifeguards ended. I leaned forward to turn it off, but Luis stopped me.

"Don't touch anything," he said.

Butch startled me when he came back out.

"Fucking done." He stared at the floor and scowled without looking up. He held the knife out in front of him and stared at it between squinting eyes. "Fucking done."

"Wash it off. Go to the bathtub and wash the blood off." Luis directed him to go back down the hallway. "I'll call my friend to wipe the place clean. We'll need to all chip in to pay him, but it's worth it."

Butch slapped his fist against my back as he turned to go back down the hallway to the bathroom. "You owe me."

"Wait a minute," Luis said. "Don't go in the bathroom. Don't wash it off. Wrap it up. We'll take it with us. We'll throw it in the lake or something. My friend will know what to do."

The bedroom door was wide open. I wanted to run in there and somehow save the girl. Call 911. Anything. But at the same time, I knew it was too late. A chill passed through my spine. I just wanted to run as far away as I could from that house.

"Let's get out of here," I said. "This is fucked up."

"You're in this with us." Butch jabbed his finger in the air toward me. "It's your fucking fault. You brought us here. You owe me big for getting us out of this bullshit."

Butch started wrapping the knife in a kitchen towel next to the stove when the front door swung open.

David stepped inside with Emily and Zoey hanging on his shoulders. Three more girls followed behind them dressed in black leather outfits. He walked in with a grin and locked the door behind himself.

David glanced to the girls. "I told you they wouldn't leave."

Emily dropped her hands away from David and winked at me.

"We've come back for you, gentlemen," David said. "Did you think we forgot about you?"

"You were gone a long time," Luis said. "We thought you might not come back."

"And yet you waited. Good for you." David glanced toward the kitchen. "I see you've made yourselves at home."

Butch stepped forward and unwrapped the knife. "Get away from the door."

David chuckled. "Did you use that on Cassandra? She's the woman in the back room tied to the bed. It appears that you have. What a shame."

"I'll use it on you if you don't get out of my way."

David was unfazed. He leaned in and glanced over at the three new girls. "They always surprise me. Something different happens every time. Sometimes they call the police, and sometimes they indulge themselves, and sometimes they run. Different every time. What should be their punishment for killing Cassandra?"

All five women laughed and approached us. "Drain their blood."

"Excellent idea." David looked at us. "We've judged you guilty for the death of Cassandra, and since you've spilled her blood, we have no choice but to avenge her death. Let the party begin! Who's first?"

"Get out of my way." Butch lurched forward toward the door.

Zoey, David, and one of the new girls attacked him at once, each grabbing an arm or a leg until he crashed to the floor. The knife broke free and slid under a chair. Butch struggled to free himself, kicking and spitting within their grasp, but he was pinned.

Emily rushed over and blocked me while the other two girls cut off Luis's escape. Emily held both of my wrists and stared into my eyes. Her strength overwhelmed me. "Don't fight me, Jacob."

Her scent of roses disarmed me. She smiled as if she were only playing a game.

David leaned into Butch's neck and sniffed. "Yes, I was correct. We're very fortunate tonight. We've scored a virgin, and lots of blood in that large frame of yours. It will be a feast."

No way to escape through the front door, so I broke away from Emily—looking back, I realize she allowed me to run—and shot off to the bedroom where the girl lay on the bed. Nausea swept over me as I viewed the gore from the corner of my eye. Blood covered her pale body and splattered every-where—the sheets, the floor, the dresser. Luis was right. It had been a set up all along.

I scrambled up the front of the girl's dresser toward the window. I flipped the latch to open it, but Emily and Zoey raced up alongside of me. Their feet didn't touch the floor. They hovered in the air laughing for a moment before Emily grabbed my wrist and pulled me down.

"Don't be afraid, Jacob," Emily said. "Am I so ghastly to you?"

"Leave me alone. I didn't do anything to that girl."

Emily pulled me closer. "I know. It doesn't matter. Stay with me."

David and the other girls dragged Butch and Luis into the bedroom with us, then closed the door. They gathered us together on the floor and stood over us with menacing grins. Emily gazed at me with her soft green eyes.

"You spoiled our dinner." David gestured to the girl on

the bed. "I have to admit—I lied to you boys. She's not my girlfriend, but this is her place. Lovely, isn't it? A fine location for a feast. Fortunately, we have plenty of food to go around. We'll begin with you."

"Fuck—" Butch gasped as David pounced on him.

David clamped his teeth around Butch's throat and guzzled the blood that streamed into his mouth. Some blood spurted into the air and splattered across David's clothes. He laughed and moved aside so Emily and Zoey could share in the feast. Butch cried out as the color drained from his face. When they finished, a third girl jumped in and finished him off. Butch moaned one last time and a few seconds later he was dead.

I struggled to stand up. I wouldn't go through that without a fight. Emily pushed me down and whispered in my ear. "It's okay, Jacob, don't fight it. You excite me. I want to keep you for my own."

They swarmed around Luis next, but didn't start their attack until after playing with him for a few minutes. They made a game of it, giggling as they untied the ropes from the dead girl on the bed and rolled her off the side. Her lifeless body thumped to the floor.

Zoey tied Luis's wrists and ankles in the same way Cassandra had been tied.

"You sick bastards are all going to prison," Luis yelled.

The girls laughed louder.

Luis screamed until David descended on him and bit into his throat. Blood spilled over Luis's shirt as he thrashed within the restraints. David backed away a minute later, blood dripping down his chin. He grinned and closed his eyes as if overcome with ecstasy. The girls took turns with him just as they had with Butch.

They turned to me next. David approached and rested his hand on my shoulder. With his other hand he wiped away the blood from his mouth. "Well, luckily for you we've had our fill for the evening, and Emily sees something special in you. She desires to grant you freedom."

I gazed into Emily's eyes. The girl who had flirted with me only a few hours earlier now became my only hope to escape that nightmare. I shudder now to think of what would have happened to me if I had reacted differently to her advances.

"You have a choice now," David said. "You can stay here, if you'd like, and explain all of this to the police. I don't recommend it, by the way, as your DNA and rambling explanation of the truth won't satisfy them. You'd most likely rot in prison for the rest of your life if you choose that path. The other option is to come with us. Emily would like you to join our family as her partner."

Emily moved forward and grinned with blood smeared over her lips and teeth. "I'll take good care of you."

"But you need to make your choice now. What will it be?"

Emily took my hand. Her flesh was cold, but those green eyes pierced me. Magical, soft eyes.

"I'll go with you," I said.

Emily's face erupted in joy and she lurched at my neck. The pain was overwhelming when her teeth pierced me, but it only lasted for a moment before everything faded away. The transformation began and Emily cradled me in her arms throughout the process.

I don't regret my decision. After a year with Emily and my new family, I've found happiness that eludes most people. I found The One.

THE UGLY TREE

Kayla lifted the scissors to open the last box of clothes, staring out the window at the forest beyond the edge of her yard. The towering pine trees created a darkness beneath them resembling a wide opening to a cave. She would need to make sure Rainy never went in there. Her dad had warned her about wild animals in the area. Rainy wouldn't hesitate to confront them.

"What are you staring at?" Eric's voice blared behind her.

Kayla jumped and turned to the side. Eric stood only a few inches away. "Don't be a creep. You scared me."

"Can I help you unpack?"

"I'm almost done."

He walked to the window. "Why do you get the best room?"

"Because I'm older. You can have it when I go to college."

"That'll be like twenty years from now!"

Kayla rolled her eyes. "Five years, if you're lucky, dummy."

"That's an ugly tree."

Kayla walked over and stood next to him. She knew which tree he was referring to. The one in the middle of the yard with the wide trunk and narrow curling branches that twisted and spread out like tentacles. She'd never seen a tree like that before. It didn't look anything like the other pines and oaks in the area. She'd ask her dad about it—he knew all that stuff.

Running along one side of the ugly tree was a dark reddish patch of bark that stuck out a little like a bulging vein on someone's neck. Some leaves had turned brown, although it was still summer.

Eric tugged at her shirt. "Play hide and seek with me."

She jerked her arm away. "Not now."

"Play." He pulled her arm and growled.

"Fine." She sighed and moaned as she turned toward him. "You go hide."

Kayla jumped at him, and he squealed as he took off across the wood floors out into the hallway toward his room. Their stomping drew her mom from her room. She scowled as Eric ran to her, and she pushed him away.

"Why don't you play outside? It's a beautiful day. That's why we moved out of the city, so you could play outside. I have a lot of work to do."

Kayla lurched at him, and he screamed as he thundered down the stairs. She chased him out the back door where her dad was cutting wood with a chainsaw across the yard.

Rainy was nowhere in sight. Probably resting somewhere in the house. She had run around like crazy that morning, sniffing and exploring the boundaries of their enormous space. Plenty of room outside for them to goof around. She pictured herself playing catch with her dad, or maybe even target practice with her dad's handguns. Lots of trees to climb. She was the best climber—she could climb anything— or even maybe build a tree house. She'd always wanted to have one.

Her dad had created a stack of wood a few feet high already. That man was a machine. How much did they need for the winter? She'd never seen her dad cut wood before, and sweat drenched the back of his shirt.

She couldn't wait to burn some of those logs in the fireplace. One of the few things she looked forward to about the new house. She'd never had a real fireplace before.

Kayla stayed away from her dad. He was frowning and his face was damp with sweat. Better to leave him alone while he was working.

Eric stopped in the middle of the yard. "I'll count. You go hide." He closed his eyes and started counting. "One... two..."

Kayla crept through the grass and scanned the yard. Few places to hide. One ugly tree stood in the center near the house and several along the edge of the property. Eric would never find her in the dark pine forest, but she'd never go in there alone. Her parents had warned her about wild animals in the area. Even getting close to it might get her snapped up and eaten by a black bear.

She played it safe and circled around the ugly tree.

As she hunched down beside its base, she stared at the thick branch above her. A perfect spot to build a treehouse. The open section stretched out horizontally and the surrounding branches were thick—they could support what she had in mind. She imagined what it would look like. Six feet across and eight to ten feet wide, with a ladder leading up to a trap door in its floor. Her dad would build it in no time. Maybe he could finish it before winter.

Kayla watched Eric as he finished the count. He opened his eyes, and she ducked behind the tree. The forest caught her gaze again. Something moved within the darkness. Swaying branches? Or some wild animals checking out their new neighbors? She hoped whatever animals lived in there never came out. Rainy barked somewhere near the house and she shuddered.

"Keep an eye on Rainy," her mother said from the back porch. "Don't let her go into the woods."

Kayla peeked around the corner. Eric was facing back toward their mom. Rainy charged around the backyard like a madman twice before stopping near her hiding spot behind the ugly tree. Rainy ignored her and instead growled and barked at the tree. She jumped at the wide trunk, scratching it with her claws.

"Rainy, what's gotten into you?" her mom's voice called from near the house.

Rainy barked and continued clawing at the trunk.

Eric walked around the tree and pointed his finger at Rainy. "Rainy, stop that. You can't bite it."

The dog barked several more times, glancing between them and the tree.

Eric wasn't even looking for her anymore. He patted Rainy's head to calm her down.

Kayla grabbed onto Rainy's leash. Maybe something in the tree? She peered up into the branches. No sign of animals. Maybe a squirrel? "Do you see something, girl? What do you see?"

Kayla pulled at her leash, but she broke free and circled around to the other side. Kayla hurried around with her. Before she could grab her leash again, Rainy squatted near the base of the tree and peed.

Kayla rolled her eyes. "No. What are you doing? Don't do that."

Eric laughed. He came over and tapped Kayla on her back. "I found you."

"I wasn't hiding."

"My turn."

He ran off without waiting for her to acknowledge that she would play. His feet thumped across the grass in a zigzag as he scoured out a hiding spot. She started counting out loud with her hands over her face, but kept one eye clear so she could watch her dad slice apart tree limbs with his chainsaw. Her dad cut through the pieces in no time at all, even the larger ones.

"One... two... three..." She finished the count and opened her eyes, turning to look for Eric. "Ready or not, here I come."

With her dad's chainsaw buzzing louder now, she searched for her brother. He wasn't around the ugly tree, so he had to be hiding behind one of three trees at the far end of the yard.

She hurried over in that direction. "Where did he go?" she called out in a playful tone. "Is he out in the forest? I hope not. The monsters will get him."

He giggled from behind one tree.

"Is he behind the tall grass?"

"No," he whispered.

Kayla grinned and followed his voice over to one tree. She lurched around the side, holding up clawed fingers as if to attack him. "I found you." She growled.

He screamed and laughed. "It's my turn now."

Her dad's chainsaw revved down and a piece of wood thumped into the pile.

Rainy let out a high-pitched squeal from near the house, then silenced.

Kayla turned back toward the house. Rainy was gone. She scanned the edge of the yard, expecting her dog to charge out into the open. Maybe she'd run into one of those wild animals her parents had talked about. Something bad had happened.

"Rainy?" Kayla yelled.

Her dad started up the chainsaw and started cutting wood again. If he'd heard Rainy's painful yelp, he wasn't reacting.

Kayla walked toward the house with Eric at her side. "Rainy?"

Nothing.

"What happened?" Eric asked her.

"I don't know."

Rainy wasn't anywhere near her dad. She hurried toward the tree where Rainy had been growling earlier. Maybe a feral cat had attacked her.

Nowhere in sight. She made a full circle around the house before rushing in through the back door.

Her mom was busy doing the dishes in the kitchen.

"Mom," she asked, "what was that noise?"

"What noise?"

"Rainy made a weird sound, like she got hurt."

"I didn't hear it. Isn't she outside?"

"I can't find her."

She groaned. "I hope she didn't run into the woods. I guess we'll need to put up a fence around the yard."

"She yelped near the house somewhere."

"Maybe she ran into a skunk or something. I hope she didn't run away. We don't know the neighbors yet."

"I don't see her anywhere."

"Well, she's not inside. Look out there somewhere."

Kayla rushed outside and circled the yard, calling out Rainy's name. Eric joined her. Their dad joined them after Eric pleaded for help at the brink of tears.

KAYLA GRABBED A FLASHLIGHT FROM DOWNSTAIRS AND trudged up to her room. Hours after Rainy disappeared, still no sign of her. Kayla turned off her bedroom light and opened the window to stare out on the backyard. She strained to see through the screen covering the bottom half of the window, but her light stretched out far enough over the yard to know that Rainy wasn't down there. Maybe her dog would see the light and come running. She swung the beam from side to side like a lighthouse beacon.

"Come home, Rainy."

She regretted not putting Rainy on a leash, but wasn't it cruel to tie her up with so much open space to run? She'd been cramped up in a small yard for years, so letting her go crazy in a sprawling country yard seemed like the right thing to do.

Kayla's heart ached. Even after a few hours of searching the area, she still wanted to go back out there and look for her. She didn't feel right going to sleep while Rainy was lost somewhere in the darkness all alone.

She peered into the darkness.

"Rainy?" she yelled one last time. Mosquitoes buzzed around the window screen that shielded her from their attacks.

Nothing.

She closed her window and the blind too before switching off the flashlight. Her eyes watered up, and she fought back the urge to cry. She didn't like to cry. Her dad didn't like to see her cry either, always turning away as if she was doing something wrong. She couldn't help it. Rainy had been with her as far back as she could remember. A sister, in a way.

Her stomach growled. She considered going downstairs to finish the hamburgers her mom made for her two hours earlier, but the thought of eating anything nauseated her. At supper time, she'd pushed away her plate after only a few bites. Her mom hadn't forced her to finish all her food like she normally would have.

She set the flashlight on the dresser and climbed into bed. Clenching the edge of the sheets, she stared up at the ceiling with her light on. A tear trickled across her temple and through her hair before soaking into the pillow.

Something tapped against the glass in her window.

Bugs? Sounded like a big one. Or maybe a small bird?

Another tap, and then a few more in rapid succession. A swarm of them? Lots of bugs filled a Minnesota summer. Maybe drawn to her light. She should turn it off and go to sleep.

The taps were sharp, like someone's fingertip against a desktop. Something out there really wanted to get in.

Kayla rolled out of bed and lifted the blinds. Darkness. Nothing out there except the ugly tree's branch swaying within range of her bedroom light. The limb was bare without leaves and it swayed in, tapping against her window a few more times before swinging away.

Strange. No wind all day. A few minutes earlier, everything had been calm. Maybe just a gust. Minnesota weather was weird.

The tree bent toward her again. Had it been that close to her window before?

The branches swayed closer, jabbing at the glass like a bony finger. She grabbed the flashlight, aiming the beam out over the tree and down to the yard. It stood closer now by several feet, but that was crazy, wasn't it? It didn't make any sense. She wasn't remembering it right.

The branch slapped forward, its tip cracking against the glass.

Kayla stepped back. Maybe it would break through.

She could reach out and snap it off, except the screen covered the lower window, the section that opened.

The branches swayed in again, scraping against the glass and tapping a few more times before stopping in one spot. The tip stuck, pointing at her.

Kayla inched closer and pressed her index finger against the same place the branch touched on the opposite side.

The limb darted away into the darkness.

Kayla gasped and chuckled.

The branch shot forward, striking the glass with a loud crack.

She jumped away, but the glass shattered and splashed across her floor. The branch burst in, wrapping itself around her wrist holding her flashlight. It clutched her like an angry parent, yanking her forward toward the shards hanging along the edge of the window. She stumbled forward, yanking herself back to avoid stepping on the broken fragments across the floor and along the edge of the windowsill. She pulled back as it drew her closer to the window, and she grabbed the side of her dresser to keep it from yanking her outside.

The flashlight slipped from her hand, slamming against the edge of the window before flying out through the shattered window. It thumped against the ground below. She strained and grunted as she ripped herself back a few inches at a time. Her right foot slipped forward, the tips of her toes touching the pieces of glass strewn across the floor below.

"Dad!" she screamed.

The branch yanked her again, harder this time. She clenched her teeth and struggled to keep from flying out the window. Her fingers strained to cling to the dresser.

A second branch burst in and scraped across the side of her chest as it snaked around her back and up her spine. It engulfed her. She leaned sideways, trying to drop behind the dresser to get leverage before her feet slipped further. The shards cut into the tips of her toes.

The pair of scissors on the dresser caught her attention. She let go and grabbed them, opening the blades wide as she sliced against the wood. She squeezed the scissors together as hard as she could. They cut in deep. Blood smeared over the blades and dripped to the window sill. Had it cut her? She didn't feel a thing. No, the blood came from the branch. Impossible. She crushed the blades together and clenched her teeth until the scissors sliced through. The branch holding her wrist snapped off.

She turned her head to the side. "Dad!"

With blood leaking from its wounds, the injured branch retreated out the window as she sliced at the remaining one. Drops of its blood dotted the floor, mixing in with the glass. Before she could sever off the branch, it released her and pulled back into the darkness.

Her dad ran into the room with wide eyes as she stood there holding the bloody scissors. "What's so—"

Her mom ran in a moment later. She gasped. "My God, Kayla, what happened?"

"Something attacked me."

Her dad stepped toward the window as her mom flew forward and grabbed her wrist. Her mom pulled her away from the glass on the floor.

Kayla embraced her mom as she examined Kayla's face and chest. "Are you hurt?"

"An animal?" His dad inspected the scissors in her hand, taking them away as her mom held her. "What was it? A bird?"

Kayla shook her head. "I was looking out the window for Rainy. Something broke in and attacked me." She hesitated to mention anything about the tree's attempted abduction. Her dad wouldn't believe her, anyway, and she'd get yelled at for lying.

Her mom nudged her toward the hallway. "Go to the bathroom and get washed off. Did you cut yourself with the scissors? Did it bite you?"

"I don't think so."

Her mother inspected Kayla's limbs. "There's blood on the floor. It must have cut you somewhere."

"I think I got a bloody nose," she lied. Better than trying to explain the true source of the blood.

"Did you see what kind of animal it was?"

"Not an animal. A branch from that tree broke through."

"So it wasn't an animal?" her dad asked.

Kayla shook her head. "No, just the tree."

Her dad nodded. "That makes sense. I'm sure nobody's trimmed it in a long time. The previous owners mentioned that the landscaping needed a lot of work. I'll take care of it in the morning."

Her dad was all about things making sense. He'd give Kayla "the look" if she told him anything even resembling a lie. All he wanted to hear was a rational explanation. It all needed to add up. Everything else was bullshit that pissed him off, so no point in giving him a detailed description—a red face and glaring eyes would meet her. Her dad wouldn't tolerate any nonsense. That was fine. She didn't want to talk about it, anyway.

Her dad walked over to the window and gazed at the tree outside. "I'll throw some plastic over your window for the night so the mosquitoes don't get in. Don't worry about a thing, I'll get all this cleaned up in no time. Go into the bathroom like your mom said."

Before leaving down the hallway with her mom, she caught a glance of the ugly tree. A branch waved at her through the shattered opening.

Kayla threw the hatchet against the side of the tree as her dad revved up the chainsaw on the ladder above her. The hatchet's blade stuck deep into the bark. She smirked. She'd missed the bulging vein of deep red wood running down the length of the tree, but she would get it next time. Jumping forward, she pulled out the hatchet.

A faint hum came from inside the tree. A moan?

"That hurt?" She stepped back and struck the tree again with the hatchet, this time launching it from several feet away.

Bullseye. She hit the vein right in the thickest part. The vein had grown larger since the day before, looking now like an elongated basketball-sized red grape. The bark covered it, hiding most of the red shading, but it was there. Maybe the lump was its heart.

"I'll cut your heart out."

Pulling out the blade after hitting the target a second time, another sound rumbled within its trunk. A low groan, like a stomach growling.

"Want some more?" She stepped back and launched the hatchet again, remembering its attack on her the previous night. This time, she heaved it as hard as she could.

The hatchet slammed into the same spot. The crimson color fanned out over its surface, then faded.

"How dare you try to grab me? I'll chop off all your arms."

Her dad drove the chainsaw into a branch above her. The main section of the tree angled a few inches to one side. Its branches swayed, but no wind stirred the air.

As the chainsaw ripped across the limb nearest her window, its leaves trembled. Her dad didn't seem to notice.

Kayla sneered as the chainsaw sliced through the thickest part of the branch that had grabbed her. No way would that tree mess with her again. Her grin widened as the chainsaw's pressure tore the bark from its skin. The grinding blade growled, mirroring her own anger.

Her dad stopped. "What the hell?"

A red liquid dripped down the side of the tree where the chainsaw had severed most of the limb.

"That's weird." Her dad leaned in at the cut and then continued.

More blood drained out as the chainsaw whirred louder.

More leaves rustled and branches swayed above them. How could her dad not see that?

He stopped again. "That is damn weird. I've never seen a tree do that before."

The chainsaw blasted into the wood again, and a few seconds later, the branch broke off. It plummeted to the ground several feet away from where Kayla stood gripping her hatchet. As the branch lay motionless, she walked over and kicked it. The blood continued to ooze from the open wound at the end.

"Thanks, Dad," Kayla said. "We got it."

She dragged the branch toward the wood pile so her dad could finish slicing it with the chainsaw later. A wide grin spread across her face. She gripped it by its leaves, imagining she was dragging a fallen enemy by the hair. She would enjoy watching her dad chop it up into a million little pieces.

He groaned from the top of the ladder.

"Dear God. Oh, Rainy, how did you get in there?"

Kayla's eyes widened, and she dropped the branch. She glanced around the yard. "Rainy? Where? Do you see her?"

Her dad gazed down into the center of the tree. "You better not see this. I found her. But you won't like it. This is bad, Kayla. Maybe you should go inside."

Her eyes widened. "Where is she?"

"She must have climbed up into the tree and gotten stuck. I'm so sorry, honey. She didn't survive."

Her body went numb. Rainy was dead?

Her dad groaned. "Kayla, I'll take care of this. You should really go into the house now."

She stared at the severed branch. That *thing* did it. She dropped to her knees and slammed the hatchet into its bark. Her eyes welled up with tears. She pulled the hatchet out and cracked it into the wood again and again. "I knew it. It's the tree's fault."

"It's nobody's fault. She was probably chasing a squirrel or a cat and got stuck."

Kayla's face warmed, and she stood again. Walking to the tree, she imagined its bulging red vein to be its heart. She stepped over to it and slammed the hatchet into the target with all her fury. She pulled it out and struck again. Over and over, it sliced in deeper with each thrust. She chipped away at the red wood to reveal a softer, darker interior. Almost as if blood gorged its innards.

She slammed the hatchet into the throbbing crimson pulp.

Something popped.

Blood gushed out over the bark. Gallons of it drained out, along with the body of a decomposing dog. Smaller than Rainy—it wasn't her. Thank God. A neighbor's dog? Other animals followed. A squirrel. A rabbit. A cat. Each of them flushed out in various states of decomposition. Each plopped to the ground like some monstrous animal giving birth. She'd seen dead animals before, but this sight churned her stomach. As the stench wafted across her face, she prepared to vomit.

"Get into the house, Kayla. I'm sorry."

THEY BURIED RAINY IN ONE OF THE HEAVY DUTY MOVING boxes out at the edge of the yard later that afternoon. Her dad dug the hole, lowered in the box, and covered it over, leaving a mound of black dirt that bulged above the grass.

"I promise I'll put up a real cross as soon as possible." Her dad patted the shovel on the top of the mound. "I'll need to get some better wood from the hardware store. The one you created will work fine for now. I'm sure Rainy is happy with that."

Kayla dropped to her knees next to the grave. She held

out the makeshift cross she'd pieced together only half an hour earlier—two pencils held together by wire. A bit of cardboard sat at the top with 'Rainy' written in thick black Sharpie letters across the front. She stuck her memorial into the mound of dirt, her eyes still wet.

"I can get you some of those branches I cut earlier."

"No." Kayla sneered. "No branches."

"Okay." Her dad stopped and glanced at her. "No branches. I'll get some boards from the store." Her dad walked off with the shovel. "Be back in an hour."

Eric stood at her side with his arm over her shoulder. He sniffed and hugged her. "Is Rainy in heaven?"

Kayla nodded.

"Why did Rainy climb up there?" Eric stared at the tree.

"She didn't."

"Dad said she did."

Kayla glared at the tree. "That thing grabbed her."

"What thing? Dad said she chased after a cat and got stuck. Maybe it's still up there?" Eric glanced toward the ugly tree.

"It doesn't matter. I'll cut that thing down. I don't like it. I hate it."

"The cat?"

"The tree."

"You'll cut down the whole thing?"

"All of it."

"Did you ask Dad?"

Her dad drove away in the truck, leaving her alone with her brother. Her mom was in town getting groceries.

The wind picked up, but the ugly tree remained motionless. Even the leaves didn't waver in the breeze. Something had changed. Had the thing moved closer to the house? She swallowed. No, it had rotated around so the severed limb her dad had sliced off now faced the yard. A fresh, longer branch faced her window.

"Will you play hide and seek with me again?" Eric nudged her.

She shook her head. All she wanted to do was sit beside Rainy's grave. Her mind spun with dark revenge.

Her dad had returned the chainsaw to the garage. She could operate it. Not so difficult to use. She'd watched her dad use it plenty of times. She'd cut off the remaining branches herself and leave that ugly tree with just a bloody stump. And after cutting it apart, she'd chop it up into little pieces of firewood and toss those into the fireplace herself. Did the awful thing feel pain? She hoped so. The thing might even moan again or squeal in the flames. That sounded like a brilliant idea.

Eric continued pestering her. "Play with me. Mom said you have to. We can play hide and seek now."

"Leave me alone."

"Don't be sad, let's play." Eric pulled at her arm.

She pulled back. "I said leave me alone."

"Are you going to sit there all night?"

"Yes."

"You're no fun. Just count to ten. I'll go hide and you come find me. Okay?"

Kayla rolled her eyes. "You go hide then."

She dug her fingers into the black mound of dirt over Rainy's grave. The cold earth housed the one thing in her life she loved the most. Her heart ached, and she struggled to breathe. Numbness washed over her for the second time that day.

A low moan came from somewhere near the house. She gazed at the tree as it bent toward her.

Anger swelled in her chest. She would run over there and cut that damn thing down. She glared at the ugly lumpy tree, and over to the pile of firewood her dad had cut up the previous day.

"That'll be you soon," Kayla said. "I can do a lot of damage before Dad gets home."

"Are you counting?" Eric called out from somewhere near the house.

"One... two... three..." She closed her eyes, but had no desire to play.

The afternoon sun beat down on her and a light breeze blew across her face. Her dad hadn't even let her see Rainy before dropping her into the box and sealing it.

"It's too awful," her dad had said.

After watching the decomposing animals drop from the trunk of the tree, she could imagine how awful. Lots of other poor creatures had suffered the same fate.

Nobody had explained how Rainy had gotten into the tree. Her dad wouldn't give an explanation, because none of it made sense. "Chased a cat up there," was only half an answer. "*How* did Rainy chase the cat up there?" was the other half. Her dad avoided the topic when she questioned him. Rainy couldn't climb more than a few feet, much less the ten or fifteen needed to get trapped in the spot where her dad had found her. But it made sense to him. She had just climbed up there and gotten stuck. Nonsense. *It* had grabbed Rainy, just like it had grabbed her, just like it had grabbed all those other animals. It had eaten them. But it wouldn't eat any more, because she would do something about it.

She opened her eyes again and stared at the mound of dirt in front of her. Broken sections of grass lie around the edges where her dad had tried to blend it in with the rest of the yard. She doubted anybody would talk about it ever again.

Eric cried out.

At first she didn't react, still focused on the mound of dirt in front of her. She turned toward the house, expecting her brother to be peeking out from behind his hiding spot. Maybe he'd fallen down. He was always goofing around. She didn't see him at first, but her heart raced when she did.

Eric was up in the branches of the ugly tree. Near the same spot where they'd found Rainy. The branches gripped his ankles and neck. It hoisted him upside down in the air, dragging him in through the branches and leaves toward the center.

Kayla lost her breath as she jumped up and rushed toward the house. No Mom or Dad to call for help. They wouldn't be home for at least another hour.

Eric screamed.

Kayla snatched up the hatchet lying on the ground next to the ugly tree and slammed it into the trunk. "Let my brother go!"

The thing swayed away from her and then shuddered as if a jolt of electricity had shot through it. Her dad had returned the ladder to the garage. No way up.

Eric called to her, "Kayla, help me!"

She scrambled to the garage and rushed in through the side door. Reaching for the ladder, she stopped. The chainsaw sat next to it. Cut that thing to pieces. She picked up the chainsaw—still warm. Ready to do some damage.

With the chainsaw in one hand and the hatchet in the other, she stormed outside.

The tree was gone.

A long trail of damaged grass stretched across the yard toward the forest as if a tractor had plowed the path. The tree had crawled to the edge of the woods with Eric still hanging upside down, struggling within its branches. His head wavered above the opening where her dad had found Rainy. He screamed over and over. Nobody except her to hear his cries.

Eric's shrieks tore through the air as they disappeared into the blackness of the forest.

She ran as fast as she could across the lawn toward the wall of pine trees. She slowed at the edge, listening for Eric's screams. Something had silenced his voice now.

Her heart beat faster.

The torn up lawn's path revealed their direction, but the light plummeted within the thick pines. Branches cracked ahead, but the noises faded. Too dark to determine where it had gone. All the trees looked the same.

She ran into the darkness, slamming her hatchet into every tree she passed. She listened for reactions. The thing wouldn't escape her.

"Eric!" she called out.

No answer. It couldn't have gotten far. She waited to start the chainsaw. The noise would drown out Eric's voice.

She pushed through the tall grass within the faint sunlight piercing the shifting branches overhead. She followed a trail of collapsed brush.

The thing couldn't hide forever. A gust of wind passed through and rustled the leaves. One tree swayed out of sync with the others.

That was it.

"I'll get you out, Eric." She clutched the hatchet and chainsaw tighter as a burst of sun lit up her surroundings.

She raced up to the tree and slammed the hatchet into its side.

The tree shook and groaned. One of its branches lashed down at her, knocking the hatchet into the grass.

She fired up the chainsaw. The roar of the spinning blade reverberated through her chest.

Another branch whipped across her neck and tore up the side of her face. She winced as she revved the chainsaw's motor and swung the blade around, cutting across the trunk.

Blood spewed out between the bark and spattered across her face.

She dug the blade into its body as far as she could. Something moaned deep within it, and the leaves rattled overhead. Blood seeped out. Maybe it would bleed to death, but time was running out. She didn't see Eric anywhere. He could only be stuck in its grasp. If she could climb up, she could pull him out. No chance.

The tree backed away. She followed it.

"Let my brother go!"

Her heart raced as she pressed the chainsaw against the trunk with all her strength. More blood spewed from the cuts, and the branches whipped at her face as it moved back again several feet.

She glimpsed its legs. Splayed roots stretched out like tentacles.

It couldn't run away without legs. She dropped to her knees and sliced the chainsaw's blade through anything that moved. More moans boomed from deep within the tree.

A branch whipped around and knocked the chainsaw from her hand. The same branch swung back and slammed into her side, toppling her into the weeds. Before she could recover and retrieve the chainsaw, another branch stretched down. It gripped the chainsaw's handle, lifting it high into the air over her.

The revving engine barreled down at her. The blade slashed into the soil inches from her face.

She rolled out of the way and scrambled toward the hatchet.

The chainsaw whizzed past her ears, smashing into a tree beside her. The chainsaw's engine popped. Sparks rained over the brush as the motor sputtered before smoke poured out. A burst of flames exploded over the surrounding trees and the ugly tree dropped its weapon.

Kayla clutched the hatchet and stumbled back toward the thing's legs as they sprouted beneath it. The tree lumbered ahead, despite its injured legs, and rumbled toward the back of the forest. She lifted the hatchet and attacked.

She let out a flood of curses while chopping away at the bark. Beneath its crusty surface was a smooth black skin. She didn't stop. She hacked harder, faster, even as the tree jabbed a branch into her rib cage. A rush of pain surged through her, but she continued. It wouldn't get away.

Her hands ached as she pounded the blade through its skin. Another gush of blood splashed out. Above her, Eric's shoe and lower leg hung limp over the edge of the main trunk.

Eric moaned.

The fire spread through the surrounding grass. Smoke filled the air.

"Eric!" Kayla crashed the blade into its body again as the tree rotated.

Its mangled open wound came into view—the same spot where dead animals had dropped out earlier. A lumpy, glassy membrane had sealed the opening and a brownish-red pus dripped across the bark below it. Beneath the membrane, the tree pulsed. A clear shot to its innards.

She swung the hatchet toward the wound, but the tree turned, her blade landing inches away from her target. A branch lashed across her face as she pulled the hatchet back and circled around to face the wound again. She pitched the blade in harder this time, crying out until it hit her target.

The blade sank deep into the soft center of the tree. The tree let out a guttural moan that vibrated her body.

Kayla left the hatchet planted in its bowels and stepped back. The tree toppled toward her.

She scrambled out of the way as it crashed down around

her. Its branches exploded under its massive weight and the ground rumbled when the trunk hit.

Within the crash, Eric broke free, bouncing a few feet into the air before landing in the brush several feet away.

Kayla staggered to her feet as the tree hobbled on its side toward her. Blood oozed from its broken limbs. Branches crept toward her, even as she hurried to her brother.

"Eric!"

She lifted him as the fire engulfed the nearby trees. She cradled Eric's flopping body in her arms and ran toward the exit. A thick mucus covered his face and chest.

"Wake up, Eric." Her eyes watered.

Eric coughed and gasped for air as she reached the edge of the forest.

Kayla glanced back at the tree. Within the rising flames, blood squirted from its shattered limbs like tiny explosions.

The fire consumed half the forest before the fire trucks and her parents arrived.

Kayla huddled beside Eric watching the blaze. Better than a fireplace.

Even as the firemen dampened the inferno, something within the forest shrieked like an angry old man.

Kayla grinned.

BOOK 2

CHOMPER

M ikey's eyes watered up as he sat at the edge of his bed in his pajamas. "Give him back."

Rachel stood in the doorway gripping the door handle while holding out Chomper toward him by the tip of his tail. She swung the stuffed alligator like a pendulum. "Get into bed and I'll give him to you."

Mikey did as he was told and pulled the sheets up to his chest. He stretched out his arms. "Now give him back."

"You're too old to have a stuffed animal, anyway." She pulled Chomper away. "Maybe I'll throw him out."

Mikey threw off his blankets and lurched to his feet. "No!"

Rachel pointed at the bed. "Get back there."

"I *was* in bed. You better not throw him out. You're mean." He climbed onto the mattress, but didn't cover up.

She glared at him. "You're such a baby, Mikey. Here's your stupid doll." Rachel hurled Chomper over her shoulder at him like a football. Chomper landed near the headboard and Mikey plucked him up before he could roll off.

He'd gotten the stuffed animal for Christmas the previous

year after prodding his parents for weeks following a trip to the Science Center. He hugged the alligator against his chest as if it might have gotten injured, then dropped back onto his pillow.

"Close your eyes," Rachel scolded, "and don't make any noise or I'll take Chomper away again. Got it?"

Mikey sneered at Rachel and opened his mouth to say something then closed it. He'd learned from past confrontations with her to keep his mouth shut. Rachel was nuts with a capital 'N'.

She slammed his bedroom door and hurried downstairs.

Music thumped through the floor. It wouldn't stop until at least midnight—an hour before his parents would get home. Rachel's friends would clear out all the beer and mess. She never got caught. He doubted his parents even cared if she invited friends over, anyway. They believed everything she told them. She could do anything she wanted.

His parents were out at the bar again celebrating *another* friend's birthday. Almost every weekend they celebrated something—a friend's new job, a birthday, a wedding. They would come home rowdy and drunk, say goodbye to Rachel, then go to bed without checking on him. The same routine every night she babysat.

Mikey pulled the pillow in over his ears. How was he supposed to sleep with all that noise? Rachel and her friends partied downstairs while they expected him to just magically fall asleep. She hadn't even read him a story like her parents had requested. She wasn't doing her job at all. On top of everything, it was only 8 o'clock. Not even dark yet. The red glow of the sunset peeked through his blinds. Kindergartners went to bed at 8 o'clock, not him.

Worst babysitter in the world.

He would tell his parents about all the awful things Rachel did if it would do any good, but it wouldn't. Rachel was an angel in their eyes. That charming girl from church who always smiled and sweet-talked them. Just a big scam. They wouldn't believe him even if he took pictures. And he *had* taken some interesting pictures of her friends with his parents' digital camera—drunk on the couch, snooping through his parents' bedroom—but she'd forced him to delete them. Any attempt to get her in trouble would backfire. She'd be back in power again the next weekend to have her revenge. Maybe even put him to bed at 6 o'clock.

He turned on his side, facing into the fading light coming in through his window. He'd much rather be outside playing with his friends. No need for a babysitter, anyway. He was ten years old—old enough to take care of himself. She'd even taken the power cord for his computer, claiming that he'd be up all night playing games—which was true—if she let him use it. Still, it wasn't fair.

Locked in his room like an animal.

A low growl rumbled from his closet.

He froze and stared at his closet door. The music still boomed downstairs. Maybe something had fallen over.

Something thumped inside the closet as if a heavy box had hit the floor.

The loud music was shaking the walls. Rachel's friends would destroy the house. Maybe if they wrecked something valuable, his parents would get a different babysitter.

The door handle rattled.

The music couldn't do that, could it? He held his breath and fixed his gaze on the door. Was someone in there? Mikey's heartbeat raced and his eyes stretched wide open.

The handle turned.

His heart beat faster. He squeezed Chomper closer to his chest.

The door latch clicked, and the door squeaked open two

inches, revealing the thick darkness within. His skin crawled. It was watching him.

"Who's there?" Mikey's words hung in the air unanswered.

He lifted Chomper up and moved him out in front of his face. Chomper wouldn't let anything bad happen to him. Whatever was in there would get eaten up if anyone dared to come near him.

He waited to see the thing emerge. Nothing came out. Either Chomper had scared it away or it wasn't anything. His closet door never shut tight, anyway.

But the door handle had turned.

The thumping music from downstairs must have rattled it open... or whatever was hiding in his closet.

He wasn't a baby, but he wasn't about to get up and close it. That's how *they* got you. The monsters. They would lure you out of bed and grab you before you could scream. The ones under your bed would clamp onto your ankles before dragging you down and eating you alive. The ones in the closet would devour you with razor gnashing teeth. If Mikey even got his fingers near that door handle, its claw would swing around and grab his wrist. It would drag him in before he knew what was happening.

He stayed in bed and pulled the sheet up just under his line of sight. Chomper stayed out in the open air to keep an eye on things. He could handle anything that approached.

Mikey couldn't look away from the narrow black opening staring back at him. The shadows churned, but no monster... yet.

Something thumped in his closet again.

This time there was no doubt. Something *alive* had knocked against his closet wall. Mikey didn't move.

But how could someone have gotten in there? He would have seen them. It didn't make sense. Impossible.

The bathroom was behind the wall of his closet. The

pipes rattled and whooshed after a toilet flush, so maybe one of Rachel's drunk friends had crept upstairs without him noticing to use the bathroom. It didn't matter that nobody was allowed upstairs. Rachel's friends sometimes snuck into his parents' bedroom and goofed around with the door closed. He cringed thinking about all the things they might have done in there.

The wood floor creaked and his clothes hangars clicked together. Definitely not the plumbing this time. Something was in there. It rustled against his shirts and scraped against the wall—its claw?

His ears picked up every noise, and each breath puffed in and out through his open mouth.

Despite the blankets covering him, an icy chill swept through his body. If something came out, he would scream.

A door slammed at the end of the hallway.

Mikey shuddered.

Muffled laughter followed. Two of Rachel's friends had come upstairs. A guy and a girl. They'd gone into his parents' room. Rachel would be in big trouble if his parents knew what was going on.

At least someone would be nearby to hear him scream if something stepped out of his closet.

The closet door creaked wider and every muscle tensed. He pulled the edge of his blankets closer. He shivered and held his breath.

A strange odor filled his room. A stench that reminded him of a country field in the springtime after the farmer covered it with manure. No, worse than that. More like a rotting dead animal. He winced.

Cool air touched his toes. They were sticking out.

He yanked his feet back from the edge of the blankets. It could have gotten him. Luckily, he'd noticed it in time. He pulled them in a little further, just to make sure the sheets fully protected him.

The dark opening widened further as a footstep thumped onto the carpet. With his view of the floor blocked by the blanket, his imagination ran wild. A thousand horrible nightmares flashed through his mind. He imagined some heavy beast with salivating fangs waiting to pounce after he let his guard down.

Something scratched against the wood door like heavy fingernails. Maybe one of Rachel's friends was playing a trick on him. It wouldn't surprise him if someone jumped out and laughed while he screamed.

"You can't scare me," he whispered. He trembled, wishing whatever was in there would get it over with. It wasn't funny at all. His skin tingled as his muscles tensed.

The door creaked open a little more but he couldn't look away. He fixed his gaze on the shadows shifting in the darkness.

The thing in the darkness moved forward.

Mikey's heart thumped so hard he was sure it would explode. He pressed his eyelids shut and pulled the sheet up over his head, bringing Chomper down with him this time beneath the safety of the blankets.

Another thump on the floor. The party music? No, the thing was coming out. The door creaked again and the thing's foot hit the floor a little closer. It dragged its feet along the carpet between each step as if it couldn't lift them all the way.

If he looked out at that moment he would see it for sure. He couldn't move even if he wanted to. And he didn't want to. If he looked at it, he would die.

Play dead and lay still. His only way out.

The air beneath his sheets filled with his hot breath. Not a single opening around the edges of his sheets. He was safe.

The intruder's breath snorted in and out through its deep

throaty gargling as if it were struggling to breathe. Not human. No human breathes like that. It sniffed again and again, like a dog on the trail of its prey. The thing smacked its lips, then chomped and slurped as if it anticipated eating a meal soon.

Within the darkness beneath the sheets, Mikey followed its movements as it approached.

The thing bumped his bed. He clutched Chomper tighter. If he could just stay still, the thing would leave him alone. It couldn't get him beneath the blankets.

With the sheets pulled like a tent over his face, something scraped against the sheets. A claw dragged its nails up toward his head as if searching for an opening to dig in at him. It moved up around his head, scratching in a wide circle over his forehead as if drawing a target. Each breath gurgled in and out as it hovered over him.

If it got any closer, he would scream.

He tried to hold his breath, but he gasped and a chill ran up his spine. Maybe it had heard him.

Go away. Go away. Go away.

Its claws moved up and dragged along the side of his head.

It would get him any second.

He had to do something.

He drew in a deep breath and screamed. "Go away!" His voice deafened him for a moment beneath the blankets.

He thrust Chomper up into the cool bedroom air with his eyes still sealed shut. His right fist slammed against its flesh. Cold, moist, and solid, like a crab's shell.

The thing recoiled as he lifted Chomper with his other hand and shook him in the air toward the beast.

He wanted to jump out of there and run, but his legs didn't respond. All he could do was scream.

"Rachel!"

He screamed louder this time. The thing stumbled back and knocked against his desk. His trophies clanked together and his desk chair spun around.

He cracked his eyes open for a moment. The inky silhouette of a tall, wide creature stood a few feet away.

Mikey growled, waving Chomper higher into the air.

Instead of running away, the thing lumbered toward him again and clawed at his legs.

He clamped his eyes shut again. He couldn't look. If he saw the thing's face, the terror would kill him. In the darkness, he kicked his feet as hard as he could, slamming his toes into a larger section of its body, a softer, fleshy surface like its abdomen. The thing groaned and snorted. Not human at all. He screamed again and thrashed his legs into the air. He pulled the blankets up to his neck and turned his face away.

While gripping Chomper, he slammed his knee up against the thing's boney upper body shell. Pain shot through his leg, but the thing moaned like a tortured bear. Mikey had hurt it. Good.

But it still didn't back away. It smacked its lips again as if prepping to take a bite out of him at any moment.

Where the hell was the babysitter? Mikey screamed again.

"Rachel! Where the hell are you?"

His face warmed as he aimed his voice at his bedroom door.

"Dammit, Rachel, get in here!"

Mikey kicked again and his bare leg poked out from beneath the sheets, brushing against the thing's claw.

It clutched his ankle and squeezed, lifting his foot toward its slobbering mouth. Mikey couldn't break free. It twisted his leg around, bending it at an odd angle. His leg would snap off it didn't let go. Far from human, that thing could rip him to shreds.

Rachel yelled a torrent of swear words as she stomped up the stairs.

The thing stopped and its grip on his leg loosened.

Michael still pressed his eyes shut, even as the thing moved away from him toward the closet.

Chomper must have scared it away. Mikey shook the animal in the air again and growled, before pulling the blankets over his face again. He nursed his aching leg.

The thing shook the floor as it rumbled back into the closet and latched the door shut.

Rachel stormed in a moment later and flipped on the light. Even after she entered the room, Mikey screamed again, just to make sure she understood it was an emergency.

"What the hell?" she yelled. "What's so damn important?"

He didn't come out from under the blankets. "Get that thing away from me!"

"Get what away from you?"

"That thing."

"What are you talking about? Why are you freaking out?"

Mikey trembled beneath the sheets. His fingers grasped the edges even as the babysitter stepped closer. He couldn't lower his defenses, even if Rachel was there.

"What are you hiding for?" She yanked back his sheets. "What the hell, Mikey? You have a nightmare? The monster under your bed is coming to get you? Well, that's what happens to naughty kids who don't go to sleep on time. They get eaten up by monsters." Rachel made chomping noises. "You better not scream anymore or it'll feast on your little crybaby brain."

Mikey peeked out over the blankets. The closet door was closed, and Rachel stood above him with her arms folded over her chest. His desk chair now faced backwards. His trophies had shifted. "There's something in my closet. Get rid of it."

Rachel growled. "Good God. There's nothing in your closet, you loser. Go back to bed."

"Yes, there is. You don't believe me, but go see for yourself."

She scowled and rolled her eyes as she stomped over to the closet door. Mikey gasped and pulled up the sheets again to the rim of his nose as she opened the door. This time, he forced himself to face whatever lay inside. If the thing was still hungry, it would grab her first, giving him enough time to run away. That would be okay with him.

Mikey held his breath as she poked her head into the closet. He imagined the thing would jump out, take a bite out of her, and drag her inside to consume her in private, but nothing happened.

"Nope," she said. "Nothing here except your stinky clothes. You're just a baby. You don't still believe in monsters, do you? Babies believe in things like that."

"Check behind my clothes."

She mumbled and pushed back a wide section of his shirts. The hangers clicked together, and she stepped back out of the way so he could see the closet was empty. "No monsters."

He pointed down. "Maybe under my stuff."

She let out an exasperated sigh and dug through some clutter around the floor. "Nothing. Maybe you got rats in here. Wouldn't surprise me at all. It's a pig sty. Shit every-where." She lifted out the half eaten peanut butter and jelly sandwich he'd left in their days, or maybe weeks, earlier. "Plenty of food for rodents in your room. Next time I babysit you will clean all this crap up."

Mikey gazed at the empty closet. "It came out and then ran back in."

She grumbled. "You better stop with all the monster talk. You need to grow up."

But Rachel was right. It wasn't there. So where had it gone? It had disappeared. How could it have escaped in those few seconds without making any noise? Had he imagined the entire thing? But it *had* grabbed him. His ankle ached from where it had caught him.

"It's got to be in there. It came out—"

Rachel glared at him. "What did it look like?"

"I didn't see it very well. I was hiding under my sheets."

She sighed. "I don't have time for this, doofus. I can't be running up here every time you have a nasty dream. Just go back to sleep, or I'll tell your mom and dad you stayed up late."

"I'll tell Mom and Dad you had a party."

Rachel sneered and took a step forward. "You don't want to mess with me, kid. If I have to come up here again tonight, no more video games or watching TV or anything. Just remember that, smart ass."

Mikey clenched his teeth and looked away.

Rachel walked back toward the hallway, leaving the closet door wide open. "Go to sleep or you'll be in big trouble. I can't handle your little bouts of dementia right now."

"It was here, right next to me."

"You didn't see anything. It wasn't real. Don't you dare bother me again. I'm busy."

Rachel flipped off the light.

"Wait," he called out.

"What?" she yelled back.

"You didn't close the closet door."

She growled louder. "God, you're such a baby. Do you need your diapers changed too?" Rachel stomped over to the closet door and slammed it shut. "There! The little monster can't come out and get you now, right? Are you good?" She didn't wait for his answer before storming out of the room, slamming the bedroom door shut behind her.

She burst out swearing all the way down the hall. Rachel always swore, but now she didn't hold back. Every dirty word that would get him in big trouble with his parents, and some new ones he'd never heard before. She blurted them out over and over.

Rachel's footsteps pounded down the stairs as she yelled to her friends. "The kid's a big baby. What am I supposed to do? He's got monsters in his closet."

Her friends laughed, then cheered as someone cranked up the volume on his dad's stereo system.

"You're mean." Mikey hunkered down again beneath his sheets.

He wasn't a big baby. She shouldn't treat him like that. It wasn't so easy to fall asleep with that thing in his closet. She should try it if she thought it was so easy.

The creature thumped against the wall in his closet again. Mikey's heart pounded this time. It was back.

The closet latch clicked open and Mikey pulled the sheets up again to the bottom of his eyes. The door creaked wider as a flowing black shadow crept down from his closet's ceiling.

So that's where it had been hiding.

Rachel had been right under it. Too bad it hadn't dropped on her head when it had the chance. It could have eaten her instead of him, but now the thing was still hungry, and it would finish its meal.

Mikey sank into his bed as far as he could and covered himself up again. He squeezed Chomper against his chest in the darkness beneath his sheets and held back a scream. No point in screaming for help anymore. Rachel wouldn't show up a second time, anyway. She'd just laugh downstairs with her friends. His pulse pounded in his ears.

Oh, God, make that thing go away.

He could run, but his legs were shaking. And it was too

late. It would see him jump out of bed and catch him for sure. He needed to keep still, but he shivered.

The creature knocked against his shirts, then thudded to the floor. No chance of anyone downstairs hearing anything while the music blared.

The thing came right back over to his bed, still smacking its lips and chomping. It hovered over his face and its body bumped against the side of his bed.

A whimper escaped his open mouth as its claw scratched against the stretched fabric until it came to a rest on his forehead. Its flesh was like ice through the sheets. Mikey pressed back further into his pillow as another claw grabbed his arm through the sheets.

He shook. He couldn't help it.

The thing grunted.

He screamed. "Go away!"

It shifted over him.

"Go away, dammit!"

It moved in closer, sniffing near his head. What was it waiting for? The slobbering mouth noises mixed with a snarl as its claw scraped against his pillow. It peeled back his blanket. He pushed back, but he couldn't resist. He closed his eyes and prepared to die. It would get him now.

He cringed as its stinking breath puffed across his exposed skin. He wanted to gag. It pressed a claw against his forehead and clamped its other claw against his shoulder.

The thing grunted. It was laughing.

No more. He screamed. "Get away from me!"

He slammed Chomper up into its face, waving him around and kicking at the same time. The creature pressed down into Mikey's shoulder with his head still pinned to the pillow. He swung his foot up, catching it in the side of the creature's chest. A soft spot. The thing loosened its grip on him as it groaned and shook.

Mikey kicked again and again with his face turned away. He squeezed his eyes shut. The thing couldn't get him if he didn't look.

He broke free and rolled across the bed, throwing the blankets aside. The thing lunged at him as he raced toward the bedroom door. It tripped on the pile of blankets and crashed to the floor. The impact shook his room.

The music stopped downstairs. Rachel had heard the noise. He didn't care. If she took away his video games or not, he wouldn't be around to enjoy them if that thing ate him.

He reached the door as footsteps thundered up the stairs. It would piss Rachel off. Good. She would see he was telling the truth. He wasn't a baby. The thing would get her too. Rachel's friends rushed up with her. Good. They would all see it.

He opened the door and held up Chomper beside his head facing backward to defend himself from the approaching monster. He avoided looking back as the thing stood again and scrambled toward him. Scrambling into the hall, he turned the corner, and met Rachel at the top of the stairs. Her face and eyes were red. She glared at him.

"What are you doing out of bed?" she yelled. She snatched away Chomper. "You're pathetic. Still playing with dolls. No wonder you're such a loser."

"Give him back." Mikey reached for his stuffed alligator. "The monster's behind me. It'll eat me."

Rachel's friends crowded in behind her and burst into laughter.

She dangled the stuffed animal by the neck and squeezed. "There's nothing in your stupid closet. You just want to go downstairs and play games all night."

"Run! It's right behind me."

More laughs.

Rachel pretended she was choking Chomper. "Good.

Maybe it will eat you up, so I don't have to babysit your chicken shit ass anymore."

Mikey reached for his stuffed animal again. "You're hurting him."

Rachel wouldn't let go. "You want this?" She tossed it over his head back into the bathroom.

He chased after Chomper.

She slammed the bathroom door behind him.

The hallway erupted in laughter as Mikey picked up Chomper lying on the floor near the toilet and turned back toward the bathroom door.

Rachel screamed first, and then all her friends joined in.

The walls shook as the creature slammed into them. Somebody hit the bathroom door, but it didn't break in.

Mikey lurched forward and locked it.

Moments later, someone tried to get in. A boy's voice. "Let me in!"

Mikey backed away from the door.

The creature must have caught the boy by the throat because his scream was cut short. Blood oozed in under the door.

The monster's disgusting wet mouth noises filled the air. It must've been starving by the way it sounded.

"Dinner is served." Mikey listened as the screams and chaos raged in the hallway. The floor rumbled as the crowd and creature thundered down the stairs.

Mikey waited for the pounding and screaming to move away before opening the door. Three kids dead. It had ripped out their throats and strung their intestines over the railing like a Christmas decoration.

His stomach churned, and he cringed, but he'd warned them. He wanted to yell, "I told you so!", but he held back.

He crept out into the hallway and stepped around the

pools of blood. It had sprayed everywhere, even across the ceiling. Streaks of blood lined the walls.

He glanced back toward his bedroom. A fourth victim, a girl, lay limp in the far corner near his door with her arm twisted in some impossible position behind her back. She stared off into nothing with her mouth hanging open and her face white.

Mikey tiptoed his way down the stairs, following the trail of blood, and passed one of Rachel's boyfriends. She had three, now two. The boy was curled into a ball upside down and it had ripped his throat open like the others.

Mikey held Chomper out toward the boy's face and roared quietly. "I'm not a baby," he whispered.

The party music still played despite the chaos. Screams echoed through the house as Rachel's friends scrambled into the kitchen to escape out the back door. Idiots. That door's lock was messed up. It took a lot of effort to open it. Rachel must have forgotten.

Mikey glimpsed the creature from the corner of his eye. A dark, winged creature with baseball-sized black eyes. He avoided meeting its gaze.

Rachel's friends crowded toward the door, but it didn't budge. As they scrambled back in the other direction, the thing blocked their way out. They were all trapped. Their screams hurt his ears, especially the girls. Rachel's scream rose above the others and she called his name.

"Nope," he mocked, "no monsters."

At the bottom of the stairs, Mikey hurried toward the front door, the only way out. Rachel must have seen him now because she pleaded for his help. Mikey raised Chomper over his head and roared back at them as loud as he could. They stampeded toward him, trying to squirm past the creature, but it was too late. The thing cut them off.

Mikey closed the door behind himself as he ran outside.

Muffled screams filled the house. He backed away toward the street, keeping an eye on the front door in case the thing rushed out toward him. A boy threw an object through the kitchen window and tried to climb out, but the monster yanked him back in and finished him. Mikey watched their silhouettes battle the monster as he stopped at the edge of the street.

No cars anywhere, or anyone to call for help. If Rachel's friends had been lucky enough to call 9-1-1, the police wouldn't arrive in time. That thing was tearing them apart faster than opening presents on Christmas morning. Maybe the neighbors would hear the screams and call the police. Probably not though. Too far away.

Something screeched in the air above the house. A large black creature, identical to the one inside, swooped down from the sky and landed in front of his bedroom window. It clawed at the glass for a moment before breaking into his bedroom with a loud crash. It emerged a few minutes later cradling a girl in its arms. She screamed and Mikey grinned. Rachel. Her body fell limp as the thing spread out its angular wings and lifted off into the night sky.

Several more creatures arrived within minutes and flew into his bedroom window, each of them emerging minutes later with their own catch. A boy screamed as a creature pulled him outside dragging him through the window's broken glass. His screams stopped as it flew away toward the first one.

The warm night air soothed Mikey's trembling body. He glanced up the street, then started walking. His best friend lived several blocks away. It would take a long time, but he could call his parents from there. He would need a new babysitter.

TRICK AND A TREAT

Jackson's arm hurt from the weight of the candy, but it was a good hurt. An aching that surged excitement through his sugar-drenched veins. He'd done well. Better than well. Fantastic. His best year ever, although it would be his last Halloween run with his friends. The candy in his bucket rose to the top edge. Just looking at it took his breath away.

He considered stopping for a piece of chocolate. No time. More prizes were ahead.

He led his friends forward. Each of them had scored massive hauls, but he'd scored more than them. He'd taken advantage of the chaos earlier in the evening as groups of children flooded to an open house. He'd return a second, or even a third time. It didn't always work. Sometimes the adult called him out, and he'd just slink away to the next porch light. It didn't matter if the adult caught him—all just a game. A trick and a treat.

He'd chosen a vampire costume not because he loved vampires, but because no other costume was available during the week before Halloween. It worked just fine, and the best part, no mask to cover his mouth, so munching on a few treats during their run was easy. Just slip out the plastic teeth, toss in some snacks, and keep moving.

Dan's werewolf costume was the best. Realistic fur and claws. His rich parents could afford to buy him the best, so they did, even though he'd only wear the outfit one time in his life.

Emma dressed as a princess with a tiara and a full gown. She always wore princess costumes as far back as he could remember. Nobody teased her about it because she acted like one all the time every day of the year.

Tommy claimed to be a zombie, but he'd pieced it together so poorly he could have been mistaken for a homeless janitorial worker. No thought to it at all. He just messed up his hair, stuck some black teeth wax over one of his front teeth, and tore up some old clothes he'd purchased at a garage sale, but that was it. No rotting flesh or limbs falling off or any of that. Not cool. He'd gotten lucky, though. Emma offered to add some scars using a horror makeup from the previous year, so for the next hour she sat in front of Tommy, sometimes moving in only inches from his sweaty face, as we all watched the prettiest girl in Stone Hill work magic.

Sam wore a Thor costume, the same one he'd worn the previous year, but now he'd gained so much weight the thin fabric stretched to the breaking point over his chest. Like most friends, Sam didn't have a lot of money to buy a new costume. Not that it mattered anymore, anyway. Their last trick-or-treat ritual was at an end.

That realization hit Jackson hard. He'd never trick-or-treat again in his life. Never score free candy again. He had to make the most of the moment, but now it was over.

Jackson glanced back at the rows of houses they'd passed. Most had already turned off their lights. No other kids around—just them. The stillness of the night sent a wave of dread through him. Maybe they were the last trick-or-treaters in town.

They stood below the final streetlight at the edge of town. The street ended, yet a narrow gravel road extended beyond the asphalt, winding through tall grass and a black forest. A chilly, fall breeze whipped across their costumes, and leaves crackled in the surrounding trees. One light ahead in the distance caught Jackson's eye. One last house?

"There's one." Jackson pointed to the light.

"We don't have to go to every single house, Jackson." Tommy sighed.

"Yes, we do. This'll be the last time we go trick-or-treating. We'll be too old next year."

Sam held up his half-full bucket. "It's not fun anymore. We can just go buy this crap at the store."

"It's not just the candy, doofus. It's the fun. We're having fun, right?"

Nobody answered. Dan took a deep breath. "I just want to go home."

Tommy stuffed another mini Three Musketeers bar in his mouth. "I agree with Dan. My feet hurt."

"No. We can't give up now. You guys are weak. We've only been out here for two hours. Maybe you'd have more energy if you waited until you got home before scarfing down all your candy." Jackson grabbed the edge of his bucket. "Look. It's just a pile of wrappers!"

"I can't wait."

The five of them stood in the middle of the road. Not even a car in sight.

Jackson stepped toward the gravel road. "C'mon, we can't give up now."

"You're wasting your time," Tommy the zombie said. "It's some freaky old woman's house. I think she does farming or something."

"How come I didn't notice it last year?"

"We didn't come out this far last year."

"Her light is on."

"So, what," Sam the overweight Thor said. "Nobody goes out there."

"We need to collect our treat."

"She doesn't have any candy," Tommy said. "I saw her once in town. She walks with a limp, like she broke her leg. Maybe she's a pirate."

"Perfect, so she's in the Halloween spirit all year round. If her light is on for Halloween, she wants visitors."

A bellowing hum came from the forest. The crickets chirped louder in the surrounding weeds.

"I'll just wait here. You go ahead." Emma lifted her flashlight and peered it into her pink pumpkin bucket, stirring the candy around with her fingers.

"I'll stay with Emma." Dan stepped toward her.

"Me too." Sam joined them.

"Guy's, we're a team," Jackson said. "This is our last chance to get Halloween candy. Do you understand what's going on? This is your last chance to do this as a kid. We can't just walk away from this."

"We're not walking away." Tommy straightened his hair. "We'll be right here waiting for you. Get what you want, and I'll just eat a few snacks until you get back. I've never been out there and it's dark. I'd watch out for guard dogs, though."

"I can handle dogs. They love me."

"Yeah." Tommy sneered.

"Don't you have enough candy already?" Emma smirked. "Your bucket's full."

"But my pockets are empty. Plenty of room in there. Always room for more candy."

"Well, I'm not going all the way over there for one little treat. Maybe for a bunch of houses."

"Fine. Stay here and I'll get the goods. You're missing out."

The half-moon above lit the area well enough to see to the edge of the forest on both sides of the gravel road, and along with his flashlight Jackson made his way toward the light. The tall grass swallowed up the path in front of him as he trudged forward. No car had traveled that road in a long time.

He passed the edge of the forest and entered a clearing. A simple stone path wound up to the front door of a neglected single-story house. No light came through from inside the house, but curtains covered the windows.

No car. Not even a garage.

Waist-high grass and weeds surrounded the house. A weak front porch light illuminated half the lawn, and a string of lanterns hung across the roof's overhang. The roof bowed down in the center and smoke drifted up from the chimney.

A low moan, like an injured bear, echoed from the forest next to the house. He pictured a pack of wild dogs charging from around the side of the house at any moment to attack him.

His heart beat faster as he stopped at the bottom of the porch. He cleared his throat as if someone inside the house might hear him. "Excuse me? Trick or treat."

He focused on the windows. Nothing moved inside. Maybe nobody was home, but he wouldn't give up without making sure.

"If you didn't want visitors," Jackson mumbled, "you should have turned off your light."

He crept up to the front door, pulling back the squeaky screen door, and knocked. A white fabric blocked a small window in the door. He listened for footsteps inside. Complete silence. He knocked again, and the door flew open.

An old grayed-haired woman stood in the doorway. Her eyes... glowed? He shuddered and stepped back.

"What's this?" she asked.

A strange smell floated under his nose. Smoke. Candles perched on glass plates hung by chains from the ceiling, illuminating the area behind her. He cleared his throat again. "Trick or treat."

She slumped forward, standing in a loose white robe and bare feet. Her ragged gray hair drooped down over her eyes until she pushed it aside. Deep wrinkles lined her face. A circular metal star symbol hung from her string necklace.

Her eyes widened, and she smirked. "Well, you're my first customer."

Customer? What a strange thing to say, even on Halloween.

Jackson scanned the area near the doorway for a bucket of candy. "It's Halloween. Do you have any treats?"

"Oh, I'm aware of what day it is." She chuckled. "You want a treat, eh? What a shame, I was hoping to do a trick instead."

Jackson chuckled awkwardly. "If you don't have any..."

She glanced back over her shoulder. "Oh, I think I can find something. I've lived out here for thirty-two years and nobody has ever stopped by on Halloween."

"Really? Not even one kid?"

"Not one. But you're in luck. I baked a tray of monster chocolate chip cookies. Would you like one of those?"

He lost his smile. "I'm not supposed to eat anything that's not wrapped, like from a store. Do you have any Hershey's chocolate bars or a Snickers bar?"

"I'm afraid not. I don't get out to the store much. Let me get you a cookie."

She turned and limped down the hallway to a back room.

"Oh great," he mumbled, "a cookie."

He frowned and scanned her possessions. Frames dotted

the walls, but instead of paintings or pictures, they contained rows of black and white symbols, like some ancient language. He knew some Spanish words, but they didn't look Spanish. Maybe French.

Several large plants snaked up against the wall beneath the main picture window, but with the sheet blocking the sunlight, how did the plants survive?

That smell. Sweet, yet it made him gag at the same time. A mix of sugar and manure. Would the cookies taste like that? No way would he eat anything she brought him. She must not have cleaned the house in a long time. Old people lived that way.

He searched for her back in the darkness. He should just run and tell his friends she wasn't home.

"Here we go." The woman limped back to him, holding the tray of cookies. She stretched it out to him. "Pick one."

Again, that sugar and sewer smell. He hesitated, but the cookies were massive. The biggest he'd ever seen. Almost an inch thick and the size of a small plate. Huge chocolate chips covered every inch.

He leaned toward them and sniffed. Nothing unpleasant about them. Just sweet.

"You'll like these," she said with a grin.

He reached for the biggest one and pulled it away, watching her face. "Thank you. I'll just take it home."

"I know kids these days like sweets. My cookies are the sweetest thing you'll ever eat. Try it."

His mouth watered. He nodded. "Maybe just one bite."

He bit in and within seconds his head swirled. Maybe she put some weird drug in there, but it was so incredibly sweet. The best chocolate chip cookie he'd ever eaten. He wanted to devour the whole thing in that moment. He took another bite. His head reeled, and he smiled.

"Do you like it?" she asked.

"It's delicious. Can I have another one?"

"One per child."

"Can I take one for my friend? He's waiting back there." He gestured toward the main road.

She glanced over his shoulder. "He'll need to come here himself if he wants one."

He stared again at the tray of five more jumbo cookies but turned away as he took a third bite. "Thank you."

"You're welcome. Come back next year if you'd like."

Next year. He wouldn't be out for Halloween next year. Too old. But she *had* invited him. Maybe he'd take her up on it.

He hurried back to his friends. They'd be so jealous when he told them about his treat. He held it out as he approached them.

"What d'you get?" Dan asked.

"She gave you a cookie?" Tommy sneered.

"Not just a regular cookie, guys." Jackson waved it beside his head and then bit off another chunk. "This thing is so delicious."

Dan reached for it.

Jackson turned away. "Get your own."

"I'm not going in there." Dan frowned.

Jackson teased the cookie in front of Dan's face. "Even for this? It's magnificent."

"Did she put a spell on you?" Tommy asked. "I heard that woman's crazy."

"She's not crazy. She's nice. Go get one. If you don't want it, you can give it to me."

Another low moan erupted from the forest.

Dan shook his head. "I just want to go home."

Jackson took another bite of the cookie, wiping crumbs from the corner of his mouth. He closed his eyes for a moment, relishing the thick chunks of chocolate. How could anyone bake something so delicious? "You guys don't know what you're missing. You need to get in there and get one."

Tommy turned back toward town. "Come on, let's go home."

"You're leaving?" Jackson glared at them. "Are you crazy?"

They stopped.

"It's getting late, Jackson." Emma took off her tiara and hung it from the side of her pink pumpkin bucket. "My parents will be mad if I don't get home soon."

Jackson eyed their costumes. He *did* tell that old woman his friend was waiting for him. Maybe he could use them to go back and get another cookie. "You're just going to let your costumes go to waste, huh?"

"What are you talking about?" Dan asked.

He singled out Dan's werewolf costume. "You guys are about the same size as me. Lend me your costume, Dan, so I can go back in and get another one."

Dan rolled his eyes. "She'll know it's you."

"How will she know it's me? I'll wear your mask, and that outfit covers your whole body."

Dan held out his werewolf mask. "She'll recognize your voice."

"I won't say a word. I'll just nod and grab a cookie."

Dan slipped off the rest of his costume and Jackson did the same. He slipped on the fur leggings first, then the detailed main body section, then the claw gloves. He slipped on the mask last. Damp.

"Good God, Dan," Jackson spoke through the small air hole near the mouth, "you sweat a lot."

"I'm exhausted. I want to go home."

Jackson set down his bucket of candy and took off toward the old woman's house empty-handed. "I'll be right back."

He stormed up to the front door and knocked.

The woman opened the door with a broad smile. "How wonderful. Two visitors in the same day. This is amazing."

"Trick or treat," Jackson spoke in a gruff voice.

"Would you like a trick or a treat?"

"Treat."

She leaned toward him, staring into his eyes, then offered him the tray. "You must be the friend of that other boy. Did he like his cookie?"

Jackson nodded as he plucked another cookie away from her.

"Have a bite," she prodded.

He shook his head.

"You must try one bite. I know you'll like it."

"No, thank you," he said in his regular voice.

"Hmm, your voice sounds familiar. Have you been here before? Lift your mask and let me have a look at you."

"No ma'am." He spoke in a low voice again.

She leaned in closer and glared at his eyes. "I know I've seen you before. You were here a few minutes ago." She snatched the cookie out of his hands.

He stumbled back. "No."

"I know it's you. You demanded a trick or a treat, and I gave you my best treat. You tricked me in return. No more treats. This time, you'll get a trick."

Jackson turned away. He strained to find the steps of the porch through the small eye sockets in the mask. He glanced back one last time at her.

She raised the star symbol on her necklace toward him and spoke three words.

"As you are."

A flash of light burst out from the necklace and struck him in the chest. He careened down the stairs and toppled to the ground as a burning sensation flooded his body. His face tingled. His body swelled to fill his cloth outfit.

He pulled at the mask, but it wouldn't come off.

"Help me!" he cried out.

The old woman laughed.

He flopped to the side, trying to stand again as his vision spun. What had she done to him? Poison him? He spit crumbs from the edge of his mouth as his jaw stretched out beneath his eyes. His airway opened wider, pulling at the mask's fur as it clung to his skin. No more skin, only fur.

He ripped at his chest to remove the werewolf outfit, but his fingers tore against his own flesh. No more fingers, only claws. The costume disappeared, leaving only an animal's pelt that became his own.

The woman laughed from her doorway, cackling like an old hag as she still held the tray of cookies.

"What did you do to me?" Jackson yelled, but his words made no sense. Growls and grunts came out instead.

"You won't be like that for long, my dear. It's a trick. But remember not to trick an old woman next time." She closed the door on him.

He lurched forward and pounded on her door. "Help me!" Only more growls.

He scrambled away toward his friends, calling out to them as he ran faster than he'd ever run before. His feet pounded through the grass as a howl filled the air. His howl.

He caught up to them within seconds. They screamed and ran in the opposite direction, leaving the candy buckets behind.

"Hey guys, it's me," he yelled. More growling and a howl. "Where are you going? Stop!"

LITTLE GREEN ALIEN

Ben strained to see the object hovering above them. It was about a hundred feet above the treetops and the afternoon sky reflected off the surface so that from below it looked almost transparent. The only thing that gave it away was when it moved, the air rippled around it, resembling a drop of water splashing into a still pond.

John saw it first and if he hadn't received that green laser pointer from his dad a few days earlier, they might have just ignored it and moved on, but John was eager to use his new toy.

"I think I can get it." John aimed the laser at the object like firing a pistol.

Nothing happened at first.

"It's just a cloud or something. Maybe a sun dog."

"That's no sun dog. That's a UFO."

"Nothing's there."

"I got it!" John's face lit up with a wide grin. "I got that sucker."

"How can you tell?" Ben asked.

"It moved. Didn't you see it jump?"

"No." Everything looked the same, except the clouds shifted behind the strange anomaly.

"I'll do it again, so watch this time. Look for the green dot. There! I hit it again."

Ben spotted the green laser dot jittering against a murky cloud.

John bumped him and held out the laser pointer. "Here. You try."

Ben took it and aimed it into the sky at the same strange shape. The clouds shuddered when the light hit the spot. More than shuddered. They convulsed.

"You hit it too!" John patted him on the back. "Good shot!"

The shapeless form burst, revealing a solid object within it. Something was there. The object appeared in the sky above them in full view, with no environmental interference to mask it. A silver orb. It wavered sideways before coming to an abrupt stop. No smoke or fire to show they had damaged it, but it wobbled like a top near the end of its spin.

John howled with laughter. "I told you guys it was a UFO."

Ben's doubts faded. The object circled in the air, making wide arcs until it careened toward them.

"It's going to crash." Emmie pulled Ben's arm as she stepped back toward the house.

"Holy shit! I shot it down!" John laughed as the thing plummeted.

The ground shook when the object crashed into the woods at the end of the cornfield. A dark billowing cloud rose into the air. It knocked over several trees and the sound boomed through the air like a thousand shotguns had gone off at the same time.

Ben gasped.

"Get in the house." Emmie pulled Ben toward her.

John charged toward the spectacle.

"Where are you going?" Emmie called out to him.

He slowed and turned back. "Over there, to see what happened."

Emmie shook her head. "We should call the police. You better hope that's not a military plane you just shot down."

John rolled his eyes. "So what if it is? Serves them right for flying that thing over our property. Let's go!"

The dust overshadowed the forest. No sign of a fire, but someone might need help. Ben hurried along with John, and Emmie joined them. They crossed the yard and entered the cornfield. Pushing through the cornstalks toward the forest, Ben eyed the skies for any sign of military aircraft searching for the downed object. Nothing yet.

"Do you think it was a military drone?" Ben asked.

"I doubt it. Drones don't hover in one spot. I'm telling you, it's from outer space."

"No such thing." Ben pushed through the field as corn stalks whipped across his face.

"Well, I guess we'll find out then, won't we?"

"You better hope it is," Ben said, "or you're going to prison for downing a military aircraft."

"Can't prove anything." John shook his head. "No proof that I did it. *You* guys won't say a word."

"I hope the pilot's okay," Emmie said.

"The alien pilot," John corrected. "We'll take him hostage, if he survived."

"If it's really an alien," Emmie said, "how are we going to communicate with it? Maybe it'll want to kill us?"

"Of course, it'll want to kill us. We just shot down its ship. But I think it'll be dead when we get in there. That thing landed hard."

"This is just like that Roswell crash in New Mexico back in the 40s," Emmie said.

"Yep, except this time we'll get to it before the government does. We'll take pictures and post them on the internet before their goons have a chance to threaten us. This will be big news. Everyone in the world will see this."

"Do you have your cellphone?" Ben asked.

"Don't you have yours?"

"No."

"Shit, man, you always carry your cellphone. We'll have to go back to the house and get them."

"Do you think it's aliens?" Emmie asked.

"Absolutely. Be sure to grab as much tech stuff as you can after we take pictures so we can stash it away. The government will take it if we don't."

"Let's just see what it is first," Ben said.

John looked back at him. "It's aliens."

They huffed through the cornfield until coming out on the other side in front of the forest. The dust had dispersed. Still no sign of any fires ahead. No approaching government aircraft, either.

John pulled out the survival knife he carried in a scabbard at his waist. He held it up in front of him as he stepped toward the trees, as if whatever had crashed might jump out and attack him. John was big on knives. He lined the walls of his room with various swords and ancient daggers. He would pull his knife out at the first sign of trouble, whether it warranted it or not. John sliced the blade through the air.

"What are you doing?" Ben asked him.

"Getting ready to kill an alien."

"No, don't kill it," Emmie said. "If something survived the crash, you just leave it alone."

"I won't leave it alone if it attacks us."

"Just don't hurt it. Maybe it'll try to communicate with us."

"I've seen enough movies to know that aliens don't appreciate their ships being knocked out of the sky."

"That's science fiction," Ben said.

"Damn right, and now that shit just got real."

John led them into the woods, following a familiar path they'd created over years of exploring the area. At least the thing had crashed on the side of the forest with fewer trees. A lot easier to get to it.

John used his knife to hack away some stray branches that dared to block his path. He pointed. "It's over there. I can see it."

Ben couldn't see it at first. He followed John and listened for any voices or mechanical noises that might verify its origin as from Earth. The top edge of the object only appeared after they pushed through tall grass. Beyond the grass, a section of the forest floor swelled up from the impact.

John ran up to it without hesitation, holding his knife out at his side like some skilled warrior. "This is awesome. I told you it was aliens. Believe me now?"

Ben didn't answer. If it belonged to the military, they would come to claim it soon. It was an advanced aircraft. Something way beyond any high tech he'd ever seen or imagined. The craft created a small crater with most of it lodged deep into the ground. The domed top half rose to their waists and stretched out a little longer than a school bus, with tapered points at each end like a giant silver football. It had landed horizontally—*if* those points were sticking out from its sides—but it was difficult to tell which end was up. Leaves and branches dotted its surface, and it had flattened dozens of trees on its way down.

No dents or imperfections on its surface. No signs of life.

John moved within a few inches of the object, stretching out his hand to touch it.

Emmie groaned. "I wouldn't mess with that, John. Maybe it's dangerous."

"Of course it's dangerous. Alien technology is dangerous, but I'll need to explain what I saw to everyone on the planet, so I better find out."

"What if aliens crawl out of that thing and abduct us?"

"They might. And then we'll run like hell. Every man for himself."

"John, I'm your sister! You got to protect me."

"Every man for himself, Sis. Ben will protect you if he wants."

Emmie stared into Ben's eyes.

"I'll protect you," Ben said, "but it won't be aliens chasing us. It'll be government agents rounding us up."

"You still don't think this is a UFO? You're nuts." John ran his hand across the surface, then yanked it back. "Oh man. This thing's hot." He stared at his palm. Red like a bad sunburn. "The government doesn't make stuff like this."

"It's a secret spy plane, or an advanced drone." Ben studied the contours. "I bet the feds are on their way right now."

"They'll arrest us if they see us here," Emmie said.

"They might arrest us, but not because it belongs to them." John turned to Ben. "You saw how that thing moved before it came down, right? You see anything fly like that before in your life? Of course not. This thing isn't from Earth."

"Well, we don't have cameras, and I don't see any aliens, so let's get back to the house and get them before the feds show up."

John clinked his knife against its surface as he circled around to the side of it. "I'm not afraid of anything, feds or aliens. Don't you want to find out what's inside this thing? I mean, technically it landed on our property. That means it's ours."

"I think the government would disagree."

"When we get back to the house, are you going to call them?"

Ben paused. "No."

"You'll call them and rat us out, won't you?" John turned the knife toward him.

"I said no."

"Better not say anything. We need to keep this a secret as long as we can. At least, until we record it and reverse engineer their technology."

"Reverse engineer it? You're only seventeen. Did you even pass science class?"

"We'll work on it together. After we figure out how it works and record everything, then we'll post it all online before anyone can shut down the area. As soon as the news is out, the feds will storm in and take it away, just like they did at Roswell. You just know there are aliens in this thing. Do you want the feds to take the aliens away and hide the truth?"

"What do you know about Roswell?" Ben asked.

"I read three books on it."

"You don't know everything."

"Well, I know enough."

Ben grunted and stared back at the object. "It's not doing anything. If there is an alien in there, shouldn't it be coming out now?"

"Just give it some time."

"Maybe it's injured," Emmie said.

John continued tapping the tip of his blade against the surface. "Maybe I should try to cut it open."

"There're no doors." Ben moved in closer.

The surface was smooth without seams. One big hunk of

molded metal. "You want to try throwing some rocks at it? Maybe that'll get the alien to come out."

Ben moved in and pressed his palm against the metal where it tapered out to a point. He only touched the surface for a moment before pulling away. Hot like a cookie pan just taken out of the oven. Hot... like it had passed through the Earth's atmosphere. A satellite? "Do you think anybody else saw it?"

John shrugged. "If they did, they'd be rushing over in their trucks right now, but I don't see anybody. The neighbor is a mile down the road, but maybe they're not home."

The object rumbled and hummed to life. Its smooth metal surface lit up, radiating a cocoon of light.

Ben backed away, staring at the thing with wide eyes. "Something's alive in there."

John held out his knife, while Emmie grabbed a baseball bat-sized branch from the ground.

"Good," John said. "I hope it opens the door. I want to see the damn thing."

Ben stared at the mound of black dirt next to the object. A stray worm wiggled its way down toward the ground. The object's hum, like a living being vocalizing, filled the air as they stopped talking. No birds. The gentle afternoon breeze drifted through the trees. All the animals had run away or gone into hiding. Nothing was crazy enough to hang around that object, except the three of them.

"What will we do if aliens come out of it?" Emmie asked. "What would we say to them?"

"Who says they'd want to talk? They're probably hostile." John circled around to the object, peering along the edge where it met the ground and across the top. "There's got to be an opening somewhere. A door or a window."

Ben joined John's search for openings, but he was more concerned that the thing might attempt to lift off or explode.

"I feel kind of weird," Emmie said, "like something is pushing against my brain." Emmie put her palm on her forehead.

"Might be the alien doing that," John said. "Trying to get into your mind to control you. That's what they do."

"I don't like it," she said. "We should go back to the house."

"I have a better idea," John said. "Go back and get our cellphones while Ben and I wait here."

"I don't want to come back here again. I don't feel good."

"You're just scared. Don't you want to see the alien? Nothing cool ever happens in this crappy little town, and then this thing drops right in our backyard. This is so freaking awesome, Emmie. We'll be famous."

"I just want to throw up."

"Feel free." John motioned to the side. "We're in the forest. But why don't you run back to the house, get our cellphones, throw up, then hurry back out here."

"Do you want me to get your rifle?"

"That's a great idea. Better yet, no. Grab that long knife I've got hanging over my dresser. The machete. Maybe that'll come in handy."

"All right." Emmie walked away bent forward holding her head.

"Should we go back with her?" Ben asked.

"She'll be fine. What if something happens after we leave? We'd miss it."

"I don't think you should have shot it down, John."

"Geez, I was just playing around. How was I supposed to know it would drop like a rock?"

Ben stared at the craft. "You must have hit it just right. If there's a dead pilot in there, the government will figure out we had something to do with it. Maybe you shined the laser in his eyes."

"They won't figure it out because the only pilot in there is an alien, and who the hell is *he* going to tell?"

Something cracked on the object like metal striking metal, and the thin outline of a circular door a few feet across separated from the rest of the craft. The door lit up as if on fire, then disappeared. The opening stood black until something moved in the shadows within the craft.

Ben and John scrambled back and hunkered down behind some fallen trees. John gripped his knife as if ready for battle. The opening to the craft was near the ground.

John inched up and Ben pulled him back down. John scowled at him.

"Stay down," Ben whispered to him.

"I want to see it."

Ben shook his head. He glanced back to where Emmie had gone. How would they keep her safe when she returned?

The alien screeched near the open door and Ben glimpsed the top of its body as it flowed from the spaceship. An icy chill ran up his spine as he gasped. Without a doubt, an alien. It didn't walk like a human at all. Its thin gray limbs stretched out as it dropped below his line of sight.

Ben's heart raced. It would come out and find them. They needed to get back to the house.

Nothing to protect himself, except John's survival knife, and that would be no match for the thing that stepped out of the spaceship.

A sinking feeling flooded his chest. No government aircraft. This thing was much worse. Who would believe such a thing existed? He teetered on the edge of sanity as the thing screeched again and rustled through the leaves near the crash site.

The alien thumped against the ground, scratching its limbs through the dirt. It huffed out a breath as a pile of dirt flew into the air and rained down a few feet away. More exotic sounds, low moans and high-pitch screeches, filled the air as it tossed huge piles of dirt away from the ship. Was it digging itself out?

John rose, then ducked again. He moved in and whispered into Ben's ear, "It's digging a hole."

A hole for what?

Ben turned back toward where Emmie would enter the forest again. Would she come back before that thing was gone? He considered trying to get out of there and warn her, but the forest floor was littered with twigs—he'd make too much noise. If the alien was violent, they'd be an easy target.

Several more bursts of dirt shot up into the air and across the leaves and grass.

John peaked again. He stared longer this time, then gestured for Ben to look.

Ben rose and witnessed a black hole about the size of a manhole cover near the opening to the ship. More bursts of dirt blasted from the hole.

John leaned in and whispered, "That thing's working fast. Maybe it's trying to build a home."

The forest went silent for several minutes while the thing hunkered in its hole until a branch snapped behind them. Emmie had returned.

Ben gestured for her to stay down and keep quiet. She staggered as if she were drunk.

"Something's wrong with Emmie," Ben said.

John stared at the spaceship. "She's just tired."

Emmie met Ben's gaze and walked over to him holding John's machete. She dropped it on the ground near John and dug out two cell phones from her pockets.

"What's going on?" she whispered.

"It came out," Ben said. "The alien."

Her eyes widened. "It's real?" She handed Ben his cell-phone and gave John the other one.

Ben nodded.

"We should call—" Emmie grabbed his shoulder. "I don't feel good."

Ben pressed his hand to her forehead. "You've got a fever."

"Go back to the house if you can't handle it," John said, putting away his survival knife. He grabbed one of the cell phones from the ground and snapped several pictures of the spaceship. He turned to Ben and gestured at the other cell phone. "You record the video. Just film everything."

"I'll be okay." Emmie stared at the spaceship. "Where's the alien?"

"It went down that hole," Ben answered.

"Do you think it might try to eat us?"

"Probably." John stood up and stepped toward the door of the spacecraft.

"Where are you going?" Ben asked him.

"In there."

"No, John," Emmie said. "Stay away from that thing."

"I need to get a better look. Nobody will believe us unless we get good evidence."

"We can't tell anyone about this if we're dead," Ben said.

John shrugged. He crept around the trees toward the open door. Small branches cracked with each step, but nothing came up from the hole. Maybe the thing had dug so far down that it no longer heard them. He maneuvered around the hole in the ground, keeping the machete's blade between him and the hole. He gestured for them to follow him.

Ben wanted to run, but Emmie stood and wobbled forward.

"Maybe you should wait here," Ben said to her.

"I want to see too."

He put his arm around her and steadied her until they came up next to John.

John stepped toward the open door, shining the cellphone light into the spacecraft. "You guys keep an eye on that hole while I'm inside looking around."

"You're not going in there, are you?" Emmie toppled to the side, and Ben caught her.

"What's up with you?" John asked her. "Are you drunk?"

"No, John, my head really hurts now."

"Well, stay here then."

Emmie grunted and sneered at John.

"What if there's another one in there?"

"Then I'll hack it to pieces." John waved his machete.

The spacecraft's interior resembled a passenger jet without a cockpit. Thousands of tiny symbols and patterns covered the walls, none of which made any sense. Pulsing colors radiated from every direction, as if the metal in the walls were luminescent.

Not much damage from the impact, except for the surface around their feet. A section of tree had dented the craft's shell.

No flat surfaces anywhere. Or places to sit. The floor circled around so that whatever commanded the spacecraft must have maneuvered around without stepping on the wall symbols.

"Holy cow!" John lit up a mound of gray and purple flesh curled up in the corner.

Ben's heart pounded at the sight of another alien. Its baseball-sized green eyes stared back at them.

John swung the machete inches from its face. A wide, narrow mouth stretched open wider in a snarl, revealing rows of pointed teeth that resembled a shark. With the alien huddled in the corner, it was difficult to know how large it was—maybe the same size as an overweight man.

Ben's eyes went wide and his mouth dropped open. "I want to go."

"Record it." John snapped several pictures of the creature with the machete pointing at its forehead.

Ben fumbled with his cellphone. His hands trembled and his mind blanked out. He couldn't remember how to record anything or even where to start. He pressed random buttons until a red button appeared. Pressing that, he held the cellphone up toward the alien without knowing for sure if he was recording or not. The image on the screen jumped as he backed away.

"You're not scared, are you?"

"Yes."

"Look, it's injured." John focused on the far side of the creature's body. The flesh was torn apart and purple goo spilled out across the wall next to it. "This thing's not going anywhere. Just keep recording."

Ben clutched the cellphone tighter, trying to steady his hand. "Where do you think it's from?"

"Probably a million miles away. I guess there's only two of them. The one that dug the hole and then this one." John reached out his hand and touched the alien's scalp. "God, this thing feels weird."

The alien squirmed as John jabbed his finger into its flesh. The creature's legs sprawled out from under it, snaking out like tentacles, but its motions were slow. John slammed his heel down into one of them.

The creature screeched.

Ben winced. A sharp jolt of pain stabbed at the back of his neck.

John laughed, staring into the thing's eyes. "You don't like that, huh?"

"Don't hurt it," Emmie said.

"I'm not hurting it. I doubt it has nerve endings like we

do. This is an alien, remember? But it'll die, anyway. The crash ripped its body open. Just look at it." John moved out of the way so they could get a clear view. "We'll have to kill it to put it out of its misery."

Pain spiked through Ben's head. Nausea churned his stomach as he curled forward. "I don't feel good."

"You too? What's going on with you guys? Did you eat some rotten food?"

Ben touched his cheek. Hot and damp.

John frowned. "Are you going to puke?"

"Maybe."

"Do it outside."

Ben wobbled, and his head throbbed. He pressed his hand against one wall to steady himself as his gaze met the alien's green eyes. The thing was upset. Furious. He didn't know *how* he knew, but he knew. Somehow, it was communicating with him.

"Are you filming all this?"

Ben lifted the cellphone again. "I think so. What are you doing?"

John brought out his knife and brought the blade up to its eyes. "I want to see how this thing ticks."

"Don't kill it." Ben's face warmed.

"I won't kill it... yet. But I won't get a chance like this after the feds clampdown the area. Here's our chance to let the world know the truth about aliens."

John sliced the knife's blade across the side of its head as if gutting a fish. Purple goo oozed from the wound, just like the other side of its injured body.

"I don't think you should do that." Emmie pressed into Ben, then backed away toward the entrance.

John recoiled and grimaced. "Oh, that smells awful." He sniffed. "Reminds me of skinning a deer." He chuckled. "I think it's getting mad at me. Hold the phone up. Make sure you record this."

The alien shrieked and gnashed its teeth toward John's knife, but it strained to lean forward more than a few inches before falling back in place. It didn't lunge at John, or even try to get out of the way. Maybe its insides were too smashed up from the crash.

Ben stared back toward the entrance. Emmie stepped outside and looked around. She glanced at Ben, then at the hole in the ground. She gripped the side of the spaceship and rubbed her forehead.

"Maybe the other one will come back," Ben said.

"I doubt it. I bet it abandoned ship and went off to hide somewhere. They're afraid of us, don't you see that? I doubt it'll be back."

Emmie dropped to her knees and leaned forward as if to puke.

"I think Emmie's really sick," Ben said as a wave of pain pounded through his head again.

John glanced back toward her. "She'll be fine. She's a tough girl. Probably just one of those female health issues. You know what I mean?"

Ben didn't respond.

John chuckled, then turned back to the alien. "I wish we could drag it out of here and examine it out in the sunlight. I can't get a good look at it." John bent down and grabbed one of its limbs, pulling it toward the door. He strained as the creature resisted him. "This thing weighs a ton. Maybe if we get some rope and we all pull."

Emmie screamed. She staggered like a drunk person and raised her arms over her face like something was attacking her.

Ben rushed toward her. The other creature had come back.

Or maybe it had never left. A section of its body was slinking up from the hole. Its legs flowed out from under it like snakes, then hardened into slender rods like a giant spider. It slinked across the surface toward Emmie, its bulbous green eyes locked onto her. It didn't look away or blink as he approached.

Ben hooked onto Emmie's arm and yanked her toward the house, but she resisted him and turned back toward the spaceship. "John's inside."

"John," Ben yelled, "get out of there. The other one came back."

The creature inside the spaceship shrieked again. John emerged a few seconds later with purple goo dripping from his knife. He jumped toward Ben and Emmie just as the creature outside lurched at him, catching John's pant leg in one of its outstretched limbs. He kicked and broke free.

Emmie staggered toward him before collapsing.

John raced to her side and Ben tried to gather her up, lifting her head. The thing would crawl over to them soon.

"Stand up, Emmie," Ben pleaded, "we have to get out of here."

She didn't answer. Her face was pale and her eyes shot open, then rolled back up into her head as if she'd fallen asleep. A green tint covered her eyeballs. She moved her lips as if to speak, but no words came out.

Ben struggled to lift her, only raising her a few inches before his muscles gave out. Her limp body sank to the ground.

John swung his machete at the alien as it inched closer to them.

"Help me drag her out of here." Ben lifted one of her arms.

Together, they dragged Emmie by her arms through the brush toward the exit.

John smirked. "It's probably pissed off we went inside its spaceship."

Ben's vision reeled as his body weakened. "Call your dad, or call the police, or anyone."

"Yeah." John paused and took one last picture before slipping the cellphone in his pocket. "Soon."

"Emmie," Ben said, "are you okay? We need to get out of here."

Emmie moaned and blinked twice. Ben dragged her a few feet until a wave of weakness flashed through him. They stopped for a moment, and the alien paused at the same time.

John growled and lurched forward, swinging the machete at its face. He stretched out the blade as far as he could but the alien evaded him.

"Damn that thing," John said. "It's like a big insect. I just want to squash it."

"We just need to get out of here."

"Well, go then. I can handle it."

"I can't drag her out by myself. You need to help me and I'm not sure I can walk much further either."

John furrowed his brows. "What's gotten into you? You've got more muscles than me."

"I don't know." Ben could run faster than anybody in school, yet within the last few minutes his strength had drained to where he might pass out at any second. Only during the flu had he felt this bad.

He dragged Emmie a few more steps while John blocked them from its attacks. John gave up and jumped around, grabbing Emmie's other arm. They dragged her along as the alien stalked them all the way to the edge of the forest. At one point the machete in John's hand bumped against Emmie's shorts, smearing in a little purple alien blood. At least it wasn't her blood.

The alien shifted from side to side as it trailed them, its

head weaving around as if calculating the best angle to pounce. Its long slender limbs navigated the brush with ease.

As they reached the edge of the forest and moved out into the sunlight, the alien stopped and peered at them within the shade of the trees.

"Get it out into the sunlight," Ben said. "I think it doesn't want to come out."

They moved Emmie away from the trees, close to the cornfield, and Ben dropped beside her.

John stepped toward it and lost his balance for a moment. His arms didn't whip around as fast as they did earlier. "I'll slice that thing up. Take a piece of it home with me and put it on my wall."

Ben heaved in and out each breath. "I don't think I can walk anymore."

John lifted the blade and swung it once before wobbling to the side. "What the hell is going on? Now I feel like shit too."

"It did something to us."

John glanced back and focused in on Ben's face. "What's wrong with your eyes? They're all green."

"I don't know. It's got to be that thing. It poisoned us or something. Now it's just waiting for us to die so it can eat us."

"I won't let it eat us." John faced the alien, raising the machete over his head. "Is that what you're planning? I dare you to step out here." He staggered for a moment. "Well, I guess this is all my fault. I better do something before we all die."

John charged forward and yelled at the same time. The machete's blade sliced clear through one of the creature's stick legs. The thing wobbled and screeched as its mouth widened in a snarl. Its green eyes glared down at John.

As John recovered for a second swing, Ben slumped over to his side. Something in his pocket jammed against his hip.

The laser pointer. He had put it in his pocket after the space-ship crashed. He dug it out and switched it on, aiming the beam straight at the alien. Maybe he could catch its eyes and blind it long enough for them to escape.

John's second swing came up short, and the alien moved out from the shade, standing fully in the sunlight with no harm to itself. Its bright white teeth glared in the reflected the light, and its green eyes grew wider when John jumped forward toward another of the creature's limbs.

Ben steadied his hands as the laser's green light darted across the alien's body. He turned and clawed at the grass, struggling to lift himself far enough to aim it. He struggled to keep his eyelids open. Whatever that alien had done was stronger than he was.

A shade of green covered everything around him. The clouds, the sky, Emmie. Ben's face throbbed and warmed in the sun.

The alien struck out at John, sacrificing a limb to knock the machete from his hands. The alien's purple blood spurted across the grass as John jumped to retrieve the machete. When John turned his back to it, the alien seized his legs within its bug-like claws. It dragged John kicking and screaming toward a fleshy pouch near the base of its body.

"Oh shit!" John yelled. "It got me. Grab the machete."

Ben spotted the machete, but it was out of reach.

The alien clutched John's arms and legs and shoved him into its pouch, swallowing him up within its flesh. Nausea swelled within Ben, pushing him to the edge of throwing up. The fleshy pouch bulged as John's muffled screams faded. John's hand poked out from the opening a moment before the alien thrust it back inside.

Ben eyed the machete once more and strained to reach it, but that time had passed.

He used the last of his strength to aim the laser at its eyes.

The green dot hit its target.

The alien shuddered and screeched, lashing its limbs out toward him. One leg slammed into the grass near him.

Ben hit its eyes again. Its torso wobbled as it stepped back. Purple blood oozed from its severed limbs until it turned and retreated into the forest.

Twigs snapped, and the brush rustled as it scurried away. A short time later the spacecraft lifted into the air again, hovering above him for several seconds before darting off into the sky.

Ben regained his strength within minutes after the UFO disappeared.

Emmie groaned and opened her eyes. "Where's John?"

"Gone."

Emmie sat up as something rumbled in the distance.

They focused on the sky to their right. Two black helicopters approached.

Ben dug out the cell phone from his pocket and texted the video of the alien to his dad. A moment later, a message popped up.

Message send failure.

Ben groaned as he helped Emmie to stand. "Nobody's going to believe us, except them."

BOOK 3

BAIT

"I got a great trap this time," Jake said.

"You said that," Tony said.

"I don't know why we didn't think of this before."

"You can tell me all about it when I get there. I'll be there in a minute. I'm turning onto the dirt road now."

Tony ended the call and wound through the forest to the clearing where he'd met Jake several dozen times before. The trap Jake mentioned came into view. Just a metal cage, like a massive dog kennel. A lot less impressive than Jake had made it sound.

Tony shook his head and parked the truck beside Jake's truck.

Jake walked over with a wide grin on his face. He rubbed his hands together like one of those old-fashioned TV villains scheming to pull off the perfect heist.

As soon as Tony opened his door, Jake called out to him, "What you think?"

"No Bigfoot is going to walk into that thing." Tony chuckled. "Well, maybe if he trips and falls into it."

Jake sneered at him. "What's wrong with it?"

"You know the size of a Bigfoot, right? It's too small, and any wild animal could break out of that flimsy thing. How much money did you spend on it?"

Jake glanced back at his genius idea. "I got the biggest one I could find. It won't be stuck in there for very long, anyway. We just need to get it in there and then shoot it with a tranquilizer dart. While it's asleep, we put the cage back on the trailer and haul him out of here. It's perfect."

Tony shook his head. "You didn't think this through. You should have left it on the trailer. After you capture Bigfoot in there, how will you get it back up onto the trailer? You don't have a hoist."

"You're going to help me."

"Hell with that. Do I look like I can move five hundred pounds? You know how big they are. Everybody knows those things are huge."

Jake rolled his eyes. I know what a Bigfoot looks like."

"Good, because all this crazy talk of him prancing by and just stepping into that little cage of yours is all hogwash. Those creatures are smarter than that. They won't fall for your little trap."

Jake's face turned red. "Well, none of your boring ideas have worked yet. We've been scouring these woods for weeks now without a trace of it. Where's *your* evidence? This is a great idea. I told you I had a backup plan, and this is it."

"I'm tracking it down the scientific way. You can't rush these things. We'll only catch him through patience and methodical steps. It takes time to collect the evidence. Bigfoot's a smart creature. It knows how to cover its tracks. Eventually, we'll get him."

"That's what you keep saying, but have you found anything yet? No."

"What the hell are you talking about? We've found plenty of stuff. Remember the cave and all those bones? Plenty of footprints, too. I bet there's more than one of them out there. It just takes patience."

"Your ideas are taking too long. We should try something else."

Tony walked past Jake to the cage. The bars were only a quarter inch thick. Plenty strong to house a pack of dogs, but nothing more. "If you leave that cage wide open out here tonight, you'll find a pissed off black bear trapped inside of it in the morning. How you going to deal with that? You got a plan?"

"Of course I've got a plan."

"Lots of black bears in the area. They're bound to go exploring your little device. How will you get it out of there? You think you'll just open the door and he'll run out and be on his way without ripping your arms off first?"

"I'll shoot him with my tranquilizer gun."

"There you go again. So then you've got a sleeping black bear stuck in your cage. Who's going to help you drag him out? Not me."

Jake folded his arms over his chest. "Maybe some guys from the bar will help me."

Tony chuckled. "They won't help us. They think we're nuts. You know how all those guys tease us. Just think what they'll say when you ask for help pulling a bear from your cage. They'll laugh at you and congratulate you on your "catch". Everyone thinks this is all a joke."

"It's not a joke."

Tony put his hand on Jake's shoulder. "We know that, but nobody will help us. Do you see what I mean? You need to think this thing through."

"Well, what were you planning to do if we caught a Bigfoot?"

"I don't want to catch him. Too much work. I just want some pictures and some video, if I can get it. That's all I'm looking for. Physical evidence would be great, but it's not practical because we don't have anyone to help us."

"Those cameras you set up are worthless. They only caught pictures of deer and wolves."

"At least we know they work. Lots of wild animals in these woods, and maybe only a few Bigfoots. One of these times it'll catch one of them red-handed. We just have to keep trying."

"My cage will work too, because I'll put Bigfoot's favorite food in there." Jake gestured toward the blue-and-white cooler sitting next to the cage. "I brought some tripe."

"Tripe? That's the dumbest idea I've ever heard. What makes you think Bigfoot likes to eat cow stomachs?"

"It'll work. The magazine had a big long article about what they eat."

"What magazine?"

"There's only one. *Bigfoot Hunter*, and the article is in issue 246. The scientists explained exactly how to make your own Bigfoot bait. My cooler is full of it."

Tony winced. "First, the guys in that Bigfoot magazine aren't scientists. Second, the only thing tripe attracts is flies. Bigfoot doesn't want to eat that crap. You should have brought some hamburgers or fried chicken. They eat the same stuff we eat. If you're going to use bait in there, think about what might attract a gorilla or a human."

"Tripe will work. You'll see. Maybe not on the first night, but I think my idea's solid." Jake nodded and grinned. "It's just like fishing, you know. Just set a good bait, and when he bites, that's when you nab him. Reel him in like a big old Northern."

"You're wasting your time with that cage." Tony shook his head. "I'll even bet you a case of beer the only thing in that cage in the morning will be a pile of rotting tripe or a pissed off black bear."

Jake looked away. "I guess we'll find out in the morning."

"I guess we will."

Jake went over to his cooler and scooped out the tripe into a plastic salad bowl. He placed the bowl in the middle of the cage and then set up the door latch so the door would snap down behind anything that tripped the snare.

He inspected it and backed away. "This'll get him."

Tony grabbed the cage's metal mesh and pulled. "These bars won't hold him—maybe a bear or a man, but not Bigfoot."

"You just wait."

"Sure, we'll see about that. I need to get my stuff from the truck."

"I'll get the rifles."

Tony turned back to his truck. "I'll get my backpack. Just a minute."

They prepared for their daily trek through the forest. Each of them carried a rifle, just in case, and strapped on a backpack full of supplies. The entire loop through the woods to each of the seven cameras took a few hours, and they would stop at the third camera to eat lunch. They'd gone through the same process every day for four weeks without a shred of definitive evidence to bring home. No pictures of a Bigfoot, yet. Nothing to spur their hopes they were onto something big. No smoking gun to verify all the sightings of Bigfoot in the area over the last fifty years.

They scoured the trees as they crossed through the forest, keeping their eyes open for broken branches and clumps of fur. Clear, well-defined footsteps were the Holy Grail of Bigfoot hunters, but even just an indentation in the soil was enough to send Tony's heart racing.

They arrived at the first camera and checked the images. Two pictures. Two deer.

"You see?" Jake nodded. "Nothing but wildlife. And that's

all we'll get with those cameras of yours. We need to do something different, something innovative, like my cage."

"Yeah, that's fine, Jake. Give that cage a shot. But I think you'll end up regretting it."

They circled around the woods, stopping at each camera with the same results. At the end of the day, the only thing they had to show for their efforts was some clumps of fur they discovered caught in some branches. No smoking gun. No footsteps either, but Tony was willing to spend months in that area, if needed.

When they returned to their trucks, Tony's heart skipped a beat. Something was in Jake's cage. Not as large as a Bigfoot, but something else. It lay on the ground as if asleep or dead. Maybe eating the tripe had killed it somehow.

Jake's face lit up, and he charged forward. "I got something! What did I tell you?"

"Probably a bear." Tony hurried behind Jake. "Don't be scaring it."

"We got a Bigfoot."

Something wasn't right. Not a bear or a wolf or a Bigfoot. The thing was too small.

Jake circled the cage and stared at the animal from all directions. "It's a Bigfoot all right. Just like in the magazines."

Tony got to the edge of the cage and peered in at the fallen animal. Its chest rose and fell. At least it was alive. Tripe was smeared across its fur and onto the ground. "It looks sick. You only put tripe in that cage, right?"

"Mostly. I stuck some sedatives in there too."

Its face was a mix between human and animal. Like some furry Neanderthal. Brown and black patches of fur covered its body. Dirt and mud covered its feet and its long slender fingers curled into claws. The ground next to the creature was torn up as if it had tried digging its way out. Its mouth was hanging open, revealing sharp white teeth.

Jake's eyes were wide, and he jumped around like a boy on Christmas morning. "I got him, Tony. I told you it would work. You owe me a case of beer."

Tony pressed his face into the metal bars to get a better look. The thing didn't look real. A miniaturized version of what a Bigfoot should look like. "It's no Bigfoot. Too small. Maybe you got one of its children."

Jake squinted at it. "Huh? If that's a baby Bigfoot, imagine the size of a normal one."

Tony scanned the surrounding woods. No sign of an adult Bigfoot.

"Maybe its parents are nearby. Maybe they're watching us right now."

Jake glanced around for a moment, then back to his prize catch. "Ah, let them watch. I won't kill it. I'm just going to take it back to town to show him off."

"We need to get that thing out of the cage."

"What are you talking about? We got the real deal here. We finally got what we've been searching for, and you just want to let it go?"

"It's just like fishing, right? You said so yourself. Catch and release."

Jake's face turned red again. "No, I'm not doing that. I caught him and now I'll be showing him off to everyone in town. This thing will make me famous. Why would I want to let it go?"

"You don't mess with a baby black bear, right? The momma bear is always nearby, ready to rip your arms off if you mess with its kid, so do you think this thing is just wandering around the forest alone?"

"You're paranoid."

"Think about it. Its parents are probably scheming right now from behind them trees on how they'll kill us."

Jake lifted his rifle to his chest and sneered at the

surrounding trees. "Just let them try."

"We need to let it go before they find him caged up like that. They'll probably be here any minute."

Jake narrowed his eyes. "You know, that's a good idea. I don't need tripe to get a Bigfoot in my cage. I got the best bait of all."

Jake smacked the butt of his rifle against the cage. The young Bigfoot gazed at them with half-open eyes, then staggered to a standing position as if it were drunk. It looked at Tony, then snarled at Jake. Its hands formed fists as it attempted to stand tall.

"You're not so tough," Jake said to it.

The animal grunted and wavered for a moment before charging at him. Jake stumbled back just as it slammed its body against the side of the cage. It strung its fingers through the metal bars and shook the whole thing.

"You can't get out of there, baby Bigfoot. We got you and we'll get your parents soon too."

The little Bigfoot thrust his arm through the bars, clawing toward Jake's face.

Jake laughed and glanced at Tony. "Look at that! It's trying to get at me."

"Don't toy with it, Jake. You'll just make it mad. How would you feel being trapped in a cage like that?"

"I wouldn't be stupid enough to climb in there to eat tripe, that's for sure. I told you it would work."

The young Bigfoot grumbled as the cage rattled, then it let out a howl like an angry man in pain. The call echoed through the air, and if its parents were nearby, they'd heard it. As the little Bigfoot raged against its captivity, its eyes burned red as if bloodshot. It gnashed its teeth, then clamped its mouth onto one bar and strained to bite its way out.

Jake howled with laughter and imitated the animal, using

his finger like one of the bars. "Aaarrr. Aaaaaarrrrr. Let me out of here."

The young Bigfoot watched him, then threw all of its weight against the metal cage between them with his hand out toward Jake's throat.

"Take some pictures, Tony. This is what we're here for. Now is your chance."

Tony dug out his cellphone and took several pictures, then recorded over a minute of video. Jake posed beyond arm's length in front of the young Bigfoot, but jumped away when it scratched its hand across his back.

His eyes went wide. "Whoa, that was a close one. Did you see that?"

"It's not happy. We should let it go."

"No way." He gestured for Tony to get closer. "You get in here too. Let's do a selfie."

"I'd rather stay back here."

"This is your opportunity to be famous. Last chance before we nab its parents."

"No, thanks."

Jake poked at it with the barrel of his rifle. "Isn't that thing freaky? He looks like a cross between a gorilla and a human. Maybe some gal snuck into the forest one night and partnered with one of those things. You know what I mean?" Jake chuckled. "Maybe this little guy is the result of some gal's wild cross-breeding experiment." Jake tapped the barrel of the rifle against the back of the little Bigfoot's hand.

It recoiled and grunted.

"Stop pissing it off, Jake. I got the pictures. We should just let him go and get out of here before the parents find him. I'll unlatch the door so we can take off. We've got everything we need."

"Take off? We haven't seen the big boys yet. That's what

we came here for, right? That's what all this fuss is about. I'm not leaving until I see the real thing. Bigfoot himself."

Tony tugged at Jake's arm. "At least go back to the truck."

"All right, I'll watch from the truck, but I'm not letting him go. I'd be crazy to let him run free before I've seen a daddy Bigfoot."

Tony nudged Jake toward the trucks. "What do you think the parents will do when they can't get him out of there?"

"I don't care. They'll be asleep after I shoot them with my tranquilizer gun."

"You better get it ready."

"It's in my truck. I don't think you understand the opportunity we have here. We just need to get one Bigfoot back to town in that cage, then everything's golden."

Jake walked back to his truck, grabbed the tranquilizer gun from his cab, then climbed into the back of the cargo bed.

Tony climbed into his truck and checked the rifle on the seat. Plenty of rounds, just in case things got messy. He had no intention of killing a creature, but he had to be prepared for anything. He slipped the key into the ignition, but left the engine off. If any problems arose, he could be out of there fast.

The young Bigfoot cried out again as it continued rattling the cage's mesh. Despite its size, that little thing was powerful. The whole cage leaned from side to side as it threw its weight against the walls. Whatever Jake had put in the tripe had made little difference. The young beast showed no signs of drowsiness. It was ready to lunge at them if they dared to release it.

Tony searched the edge of the forest for any signs of young Bigfoot's parents. Nothing out of the ordinary. Maybe its parents were waiting for them to leave before approaching. If they didn't appear within an hour, he would insist they open the cage and head home. Jake would just have to try again another time.

A booming low cry filled the air. Much louder than the young Bigfoot. Tony rolled his window down an inch to listen. Branches swayed and cracked ahead, beyond the cage. A dark figure emerged from the edge of the forest and moved out into the open. Tony's pulse pounded in his ears. It was there, about a hundred feet away—a furry, muscular frame crept toward the cage. It had the same humanoid-gorilla face as the young one. Everything Tony had ever read about the beast was true.

Its gaze locked on Tony and Jake as it advanced, lifting its hands in a defensive pose. Its arms were long and slender with patches of fur torn away in several areas as if it'd been in a recent battle. Maybe a black bear had trespassed on its territory and lost.

Instead of charging toward the cage to rescue its child, the larger Bigfoot slinked forward and crouched down as if ready to pounce on the perpetrator of the crime.

The young Bigfoot howled and stretched out its arms toward its parent. Judging from the larger Bigfoot's breasts, Tony assumed the approaching beast was the mother, which meant the father might be nearby too.

Jake caught Tony's gaze for a moment, giving him the thumbs up signal. Tony considered taking out his cellphone to record again, but his hands trembled too much and he squeezed his rifle.

The mommy reached the cage and comforted its trapped child, while glancing back at Jake and Tony. Jake lifted his tranquilizer gun over the top edge of his cargo bed and aimed. Tony swallowed and held back a desire to yell at Jake. He shouldn't shoot them, even if it was only a tranquilizer dart. Just let the mommy grab the child and go. Tony pressed his mouth shut.

Jake fired one shot, sticking the dart in the mother's lower chest. She recoiled and twisted around before knocking the dart away, but it was too late. The chemicals in the dart started doing their job. She teetered, then clutched the bars of the cage. She snarled at Jake and Tony, her eyes wide and red like her child.

"Got you!" Jake yelled. "Down you go."

The mother Bigfoot wobbled and lurched toward Jake, but toppled over a few seconds later. The young Bigfoot cried out again and shook the cage.

Jake jumped out of the cargo bed, but another Bigfoot pounced on him from out of nowhere before his feet hit the ground. It grabbed Jake by the neck and whipped him against the side of the truck.

Tony froze. It was the father Bigfoot. The one they'd dreamed of discovering for years. It was at least seven feet tall with limbs like a professional wrestler. Its narrow eyes focused on Jake, and it knocked the tranquilizer gun out of Jake's hands before he could aim it again.

Tony climbed out of his truck and fired three warning shots over the father Bigfoot's head. The beast shot a look at him that sent a chill up Jake's spine. Instead of charging at Tony, the Bigfoot grabbed Jake by the leg and dragged him toward the cage.

Jake stretched toward the tranquilizer gun, but it was far beyond his reach. He screamed and thrashed as it dragged Jake along like a rag doll. When it reached the cage, it stomped its foot down on Jake's leg, pinning him to the ground. Jake squirmed around and tried to break free, but the Bigfoot had him good.

The mother Bigfoot rose to her feet and joined her child in shaking the cage, but the effects of the tranquilizer dart prevented it from doing any damage. She clung to the cage just to keep from falling down.

Jake squirmed and hammered at the father Bigfoot's body as it dragged him to the door of the cage. It must have been watching them earlier because it forced Jake's hands against the latch to open the door as if it understood the concept of the door, but just not how to make it work.

Jake fought against it at first until the Bigfoot slammed him head-first into the door. Blood ran down Jake's face as the Bigfoot forced his hands up near the door latch again. That time, Jake opened the door. The Bigfoot held Jake by one foot as the young Bigfoot escaped the cage and ran off into the woods. The mother Bigfoot wobbled away after her child.

Jake screamed as the Bigfoot dragged him into the cage and tossed him against the back wall. The cage rattled when his body slammed into the metal mesh.

Tony lifted his rifle and aimed. That would be the perfect opportunity to take it down before it came out and attacked him, but he hesitated. He held the Bigfoot in his rifle scope as it slammed the door shut. He pressed his finger on the trigger, but didn't squeeze it.

The Bigfoot turned toward him and glared at him. With its eyes burning with hate, it grinned at him and took a step forward.

Tony's muscles tensed, but the Bigfoot stopped. It raised its chin and glanced around the area before lumbering away toward the others.

"Take it down, Tony!" Jake called from the cage. Blood covered his face and chest. "Don't let it get away!"

Tony followed the Bigfoot in his scope until it disappeared in the forest. He lowered his rifle and stepped toward the cage, but stopped.

"Tony, I'm busted up good." Jake groaned. "Why didn't you shoot that thing?"

Tony crept forward, keeping his rifle ready. He scanned

the woods and listened for branches breaking. Maybe the thing would circle around and approach him from a different angle. Catch him in a surprise attack like it had Jake.

"I'll be right there," Tony said.

"Get me out of here. You should have blasted that thing while you had the chance. We could have taken it back to town."

"I got pictures."

Jake smirked. "Pictures."

Tony moved forward a few more feet until a branch cracked in the woods to his left. He swung the barrel in that direction. Nothing there. Maybe just the breeze.

"Do you think they went home?" Jake asked. "Dammit, Tony, why the hell didn't you shoot. That thing almost killed me. What were you thinking?"

"You caged up its child, Jake. What did you think it'd do?"

Jake swore under his breath. "Just get me out of here. Are they gone?"

"I don't know."

Halfway to the cage, shadows moved within the trees to his right. Maybe just a trick of light, but maybe the Bigfoot never left. Just stalking them within the darkness, waiting for an opportunity to attack.

"Can you stand up?"

"I don't think so. My leg's busted up."

"I think they're watching us."

"Hell with that. Just blast them next time. Don't play around. You saw it almost killed me, right? I'll need some help."

"Stand up, if you can. We'll need to hurry when I open the door, so get ready to run back to the truck."

Jake smirked and groaned. "Yeah, right, run."

"Those things are watching us, Jake. I know it. You've got to stand up. If I come in there with you, I just know one of them is going to run out of the woods and lock me in there with you."

"I'll try." Jake staggered to his feet as Tony approached. Blood soaked his shirt and pants, and he clutched his stomach. "It cut my stomach open, Tony. I can feel it."

"I'll get you to a doctor as soon as we get out of here."

Jake lifted his hand for a moment. A hunk of bloody flesh poked out through his torn shirt. Jake chuckled and winced. "Look, Tony. Tripe."

Tony scanned the edge of the surrounding forest, watching for any approaching Bigfoots, but still no sign of them. He lifted the latch on the cage and stepped inside.

Jake limped toward Tony like a zombie straight out of a horror movie. Jake cringed with each step and groaned.

"I got you." Tony grabbed Jake's arm as Jake stumbled.

"Bring me over to my gun. I bet we can still nab one."

A branch cracked nearby as a Bigfoot came out of the forest. A second one followed behind him.

Tony pulled on Jake's arm. "They're coming back."

"Just get my gun." Jake gestured toward where he'd dropped it.

Tony's heart pounded as he dragged Jake out of the cage. The blood smeared across the ground and soaked into Tony's clothes as the Bigfoots approached within fifty feet of them. If they got any closer Tony would stop and fire his rifle.

"Take them down, Tony. They'll kill us if you don't."

"I got this. I think we can make it to the truck."

"Dammit, let me have your rifle then. I'll do it."

Tony paused. The two Bigfoots continued forward. The father Bigfoot was there, along with another male. How many were there? As soon as the question popped into his mind, grunting and thumping footsteps erupted behind him.

He pivoted as several more of the creatures approached, swarming out through the brush and trees. All of them were as large as the father Bigfoot, but the faces of each one displayed distinct characteristics. Some old, some young, some muscular and fierce, some weak and wise. They stormed in from all directions, every face full of anger and focus. Jake and Tony were the target of their rage.

When Tony's gaze met their eyes, a few of them charged forward. The others circled in around them as Tony dropped Jake to the ground. He brought up the rifle toward the nearest one, aiming it at its heart, but angling it up above its head to fire a few warning shots first. None of them slowed.

"You missed. Give me that thing." Jake yelled. "I'll do it."

Tony handed Jake his rifle and hurried toward his truck, scooping up Jake's tranquilizer gun along the way. Before he climbed in, he turned back. The two Bigfoot creatures reached Jake before he could bring the rifle up to fire it. They knocked his rifle away and tore at his chest, throwing him back to the ground.

"Tony," Jake said beneath the grunts of the Bigfoots tearing him open.

Tony turned and fired the tranquilizer gun at the two creatures, then shot one into Jake's chest. Blood covered his body. He wouldn't make it. Better to put him out of his misery.

As Tony climbed into the driver's seat of his truck, a Bigfoot jumped up into his cargo bed and pounded on the roof of his cab. The metal banging was deafening as Tony started the engine and threw the truck into reverse with the tranquilizer gun in his lap.

He started backing out when the driver's side window glass shattered. A pair of gorilla-like hands clutched his shirt and plucked him out of his seat.

The Bigfoot hurled him through the air and slammed him to the ground. He landed on his head, sending waves of pain surging through his spine. The tranquilizer gun crashed on the ground next to him.

Several Bigfoots swarmed in and ripped at his clothes and flesh. They tore open his chest and pulled out his intestines, dangling them in the air like spaghetti.

Tony struggled toward the tranquilizer gun. Maybe he could still get out of there. He touched the barrel, but a Bigfoot stomped its enormous foot down on it.

The Bigfoots howled as they tore out his stomach. They passed it around like a raw steak, with each one taking a big bite of it.

Jake was right. They really did like tripe.

BIRTHDAY BOY

Wesley came up with the idea to go see Dolores for his cousin's 30th birthday.

"I'm not interested," I said.

"Doesn't matter," Wesley said, "it's not for you, it's for John. What else are we gonna do for him?"

Wesley was right. Not much to do in our small Florida town except go out to the bar or stay at home and invite a bunch of friends over.

"When's his birthday?" I asked.

"Tomorrow."

"What the hell? Why didn't you tell me sooner? I would have planned something."

"No need to plan. John doesn't like big parties, anyway. Not the partying type. He won't have nothing going on. We can just take him out there and drop him off for a couple of hours. I want to do something *special* for him."

"She's special all right."

Wesley laughed. "He won't never forget Dolores."

"I haven't forgotten her, that's for sure."

"Me neither."

"You got sunglasses?"

"Two pair."

"I'm tempted not to wear them."

Wesley shook his head. "Not worth it. Better just keep them on."

"You're right."

Dolores would take John's mind off every problem he'd ever had in his life. She lived alone in the woods about an hour north of Lake Sumter.

"I bet she ain't aged a bit." Wesley held back a laugh.

"Are you sure you want to do that to him?" I asked.

"Hell yeah! Do you regret meeting her?"

The memories flooded back, and I grinned. "No."

"Well, there you go. Me neither. They'll both be whooping it up in no time after she gets Johnny in her arms."

"Maybe she's dead? It's been almost twenty years."

"She ain't dead. I drove in there a week ago, just to check —I did *not* go in, by the way—and her light was on. The place looked exactly the same as it did when we were there."

"It'll be interesting to see her again."

"Yes, it will—through our sunglasses."

The next day, Wesley drove us to her place up north of Lake Sumter to a wooded area. John sat in the backseat tapping his damn foot against the passenger side floor the whole way. He was the nervous type—never sat still.

"She's a lovely lady," Wesley said. "Just lovely."

"Why do you keep saying that?" John asked. "You think I won't like her?"

"You'll love her." Wesley winked at me.

"I saw that. What's wrong with her?"

"Nothing at all."

John insisted on wearing nice clothes and getting all dressed up, even after I told him that Dolores didn't care about that stuff. She'd love him just the way he was, but he went out and bought a new fancy blue shirt for the occasion.

"You're wasting your money," Wesley said to him. "She doesn't care what you look like. But you better bring her something, just to be nice. She loves red roses."

"How do you know what she likes?"

"I just know."

"You've been with her before?"

"I'm not gonna answer that!" Wesley laughed and glanced at me.

"Why not? She ugly?"

"No, not ugly at all, Johnny," Wesley said. "Picture the most beautiful woman in the world. That's what she looks like. That's the truth."

"I get the feeling you're not telling me something."

"You don't love beautiful women?"

"I do." John looked at Wesley suspiciously.

"That's what you're getting tonight. A beautiful woman. What the hell are you complaining for?"

"I ain't complaining."

"Good, because we drove all the way out here just for you. That'd suck if you missed this opportunity."

"We can stop and have a beer on the side of the road before we get there," I suggested, "if that would help."

I craned my neck back at John. He was shaking his head. "No, I want to make a good impression."

"There's a whole case in the trunk. We can chill out for a few minutes. Calm your nerves before we go in."

Wesley shook his head and nudged me. "Best John not drink anything before he meets her." Wesley pointed to his eyes. "It might mess with his sight, if you know what I mean."

"Yeah, I guess you're right. It's probably best you stay sober. You want to see things clearly when you take in the full spectacle of Dolores. She's a sight to behold."

I slowed down along the edge of the highway and pointed to the gravel path leading into the forest. "Her place is in there."

"Where's the road?" John asked.

"It's there. Just that path."

"We need to walk there?"

"We can drive in, but it's overgrown with weeds. Dolores doesn't get too many visitors."

"How do you know this woman, anyway?"

"I told you before. Just a friend."

"A friend from where?"

Wesley grinned and shot a glance at me. "A friend I knew in college." He chuckled.

"If she's so beautiful," John said, "why don't you marry her?"

Wesley scowled and groaned. "Dolores isn't the *marrying* type."

"Wes, you're scaring the guy."

"Sorry."

"So she dates a lot of guys?"

"As many as she can find."

"Oh," John's voice trailed off. "I get it."

"Don't get all emotional on us," I said. "You haven't met her yet. Dolores just likes to have a little fun and move on, but you may be just the guy she's looking for."

"Johnny, my boy, I'm positive you're the guy she's looking for," Wesley said.

"She ain't no prostitute, is she?" John said. "I'm not desperate."

"I know you're not. She's just affectionate. The type of woman to help a guy like you."

"What you mean a guy like me?"

Wesley shrugged. "A guy looking for someone *special*."

I smirked. "She's special all right."

Wesley knocked the back of his hand against my leg. "Don't get him thinking there's something wrong with her."

I turned back to John. "There's nothing wrong with her. As soon as you see her you'll fall in love. I'm sure of that."

"How do you know I'll fall in love if you haven't seen her in years? Maybe she's all old and ugly now?"

"Well, let me just say this. You will thank me."

Wesley steered the Cadillac onto the gravel road leading to her house. The path wound through the trees and he turned on the headlights to see where we were going. The darkness enveloped us even though the sun hadn't gone down yet. Only a few slivers of light broke through the leaves overhead.

One light lit her porch up ahead. The memories came flooding back. I'd been out to her house a few times in my college years, but nothing about her place had changed. Same old run-down shack. I pushed away the nostalgia. Time for John to have some fun.

Wesley parked the car in a clearing in front of her gate. No other cars in sight, but her garage door was closed. If she had a car, nobody had used it in years.

"This is it?" John asked.

"Yep." I grinned.

"What do I do now?"

"Don't you worry. We'll walk you up to the door," Wesley said. "You think we're just gonna drop you off in the woods and drive away?"

"Yeah."

"Hell, I wouldn't do something like that to my favorite cousin."

"Yeah, you would."

We climbed out of the car and Wesley left the engine running so the headlights would illuminate the front porch of her house. Just a single-story house with vines snaking up the siding. A white picket fence ran around the perimeter of her yard, although you could only see the top half of it because the weeds were so thick. Maybe if Dolores cleaned up the place it would look nice, but now it resembled a drug dealer's hangout.

Wesley dug into his pocket and dug out his cell phone. He jumped a few steps in front of John and started filming everything.

"What's that for?" John asked.

"You'll thank me later. I want you to remember everything."

"Oh yeah," Wesley said, "I almost forgot." Wesley took out his sunglasses, slipped them on, then handed me a pair.

"Why are you wearing those?" John asked. "Trying to hide your faces?"

"Nope. I'm sure Dolores won't have any problem recognizing us either way. We just feel more comfortable with them on."

"You bring me a pair?"

Wesley threw his arm over John's shoulder and walked him forward. "You shouldn't wear them. Let her see your baby blue eyes."

"I can barely see anything in here. Shouldn't you take them off? Maybe she'll want to see your eyes too?"

"Oh, no. We're keeping the sunglasses on. Ray and I need to look cool, you know."

"You don't need them."

"Oh, yes we do." Wesley laughed and nudged John forward. "Now, you just go in there and have yourself a good time. Dolores is a little darling. She'll treat you nice."

"Maybe I should have had that beer. I can't talk to girls. Maybe we should go back to the car and have a few."

Wesley pushed him forward. "Now, don't get all worked up before you go in there. You'll need all your strength to handle the love she'll be giving you." He swatted John's back. "Who could resist your charms?"

"Oh, I forgot the flowers." John rushed back to the car and returned with the bouquet of red roses.

"She *loves* flowers."

"Maybe I should have gotten something better."

"Flowers are perfect. Dolores will go crazy when she sees them."

John arranged the roses, then slicked back the side of his hair. "How do I look?"

"Like a handsome guy ready to meet a beautiful woman. She'll jump in your lap in no time. Just hold those flowers out when you walk up to the door. She'll be watching through the window. You want to make sure she knows your intentions." Wesley looked toward the house.

Dolores was peeking out at us between her blinds. Not a light on in the house and I couldn't see her face, but I felt her gaze like a physical touch.

"You look dapper, John," I said. "Just go in there and have a wonderful time. Don't worry about us."

"All right. Here I go."

John walked through the gate, and Wesley and I followed behind him. Wesley filmed John from the side, then moved back behind him after we reached the porch.

"Are you going to be filming the whole thing?" John asked.

Wesley peeked out from behind his cell phone. "Until you go inside. After that, it's all just between you and her."

"You're not going to post that on YouTube, are you? Try to embarrass me?"

"Nope. This is all for you, John. You'll look back on this day and remember it as being the happiest day of your life. You'll thank us for bringing you here. Trust me."

"I guess. What if she doesn't like me?"

"Stop with your nonsense. Of course she'll like you. She

will like you a lot. Now knock on that damn door and impress the little lady."

John glanced at the flowers, then at the door. "If she's ugly, I'm running back to the car."

"Stop that shit and knock."

"All right. I guess I can go in there. I guess it'll be okay."

"Sure, it will."

"Hold out those flowers," I said.

He held them out further, then formed a fist up near the door, but he didn't knock. "I'm kind of nervous."

"Take a deep breath. She's the girl of your dreams, man. She's got everything you like. Pretty hair, great figure. Sweet voice. You'll fall head over heels in love."

"What if she doesn't want me to come in?"

"She will. Just shut your mouth and give her all your love, got it?"

"What if I get in there but then mess it up? I always mess up this stuff. Remember what happened with Mary?"

"Don't you be comparing Dolores to Mary. Mary was a lunkhead. She didn't deserve you."

"You told me Mary would be the one."

"Well, I messed up with Mary. This Dolores girl is a million times better than Mary. Quality stuff. I'm telling you right now this is something you won't forget."

"What if—"

Wesley rolled his eyes and raised his voice. "Stop. I'm not telling you again. Just knock and enjoy the night. When she comes to the door, your eyes will pop out. She's the most beautiful girl in the whole world. Your dream girl."

John grunted and shifted the roses again.

Her living room blinds rustled and her face appeared in the window for a moment. Her eyes locked onto me. That's when I looked away. I got a little dizzy for a moment and grabbed onto Wesley's shoulder.

"You okay, man?" he asked.

"Yeah. She's watching us."

Wesley didn't look. He continued holding up the cell phone to record the whole thing.

"You got enough battery power in that thing?" I asked.

"Plenty. We'll be good for a couple more hours, at least."

John heaved in a deep breath, then knocked.

Dolores answered the door a few seconds later.

Her eyes darted between us and then locked onto the flowers in John's hand. "Are you boys lost?"

I cringed at the sound of her voice. I avoided looking at her face but I couldn't help glancing at her. It'd been so long and she still looked the same. She eyed me up and down. She caught me staring at her and grinned. Of course, she remembered me.

John glanced back at us for a moment. A wide grin spread across his face and his eyes were all lit up. His hands shook as he held out the roses toward Dolores.

"We came to see you, Dolores," I said. "My friend here is a bit nervous. He brought you something."

"Some flowers." John held them up closer to her face.

Dolores grabbed them and pulled them back under her nose. She sniffed every single flower, then narrowed her eyes. "What do you want?"

John glanced back to Wesley. "Oh my God. She's beautiful."

"Don't sweet talk me, idiot. Talk to her." Wesley nudged him to face Dolores.

John shifted from one foot to the other. "I was wondering if you'd like to... meet me?"

She moved a little closer to him. "Why, aren't you just the sweetest thing?" She gazed straight into Wesley's cellphone and winked. "Did you put him up to this?"

"We wanted to do something nice for him on his birthday."

"Well, it's your birthday, but you brought *me* the present. Such a handsome young man. You're more than welcome to come inside. In fact, all of you can come in, if you'd like."

Wesley chuckled, still filming every moment. "No, thanks."

She looked past John and caught my gaze. "Take off your glasses, Ray. Come inside and join the party. We had such fun together. I remember every second."

I shook my head. No way was she getting me back in there. "We'll just wait out here."

"What makes you think your friend will want to leave when I'm done with him?"

"He can't stay the night, Dolores," Wesley said, "so don't get your hopes up."

John turned to his cousin. "Why not?"

"You got to get back to your job in the morning, remember?"

"I can call in sick."

"No, you can't. You got to get back home. You come back outside when you're done. We'll be waiting for you in the car."

Dolores chuckled. "I don't think he'll want to leave. They never want to leave."

John mumbled as Dolores reached out and grabbed him by the front of his shirt, pulling him into the house. She blew me a kiss, then slammed the door.

We stood on the porch a few minutes, waiting to see if John might run out screaming, but just as we planned, everything went smoothly. Wesley shut off his video, and we headed out to the car.

"I'm not sure he'll want to leave," I said.

"We'll drag him out if we have to."

"I didn't want to leave either. Remember that?"

"I remember."

We climbed into the car and reviewed the video on the phone. Everything was there. It would have only been better if we could have filmed a little more of John and Dolores's interactions. A few seconds of them cuddling would have been hilarious.

We waited for almost two hours listening to the radio and downing a few beers out of the case in the trunk. Wesley brought up all the stupid shit we'd done in our youth. Our time with Dolores was at the top of our list. We laughed until my stomach ached.

"Maybe we shouldn't have brought John here," I said.

"Are you kidding me? He ain't never gonna forget this. If that guy ever gets married, I'll tease him about it on his wedding day."

"I feel kind of bad for him. Seems like a nice guy."

"Yeah," Wesley said. "John's a good kid. I feel a little bad for him too, but then again, it's a lesson he won't forget."

"He won't ever trust you again."

Wesley laughed. "And for good reason. Serves him right for trusting a devil like me."

"Let's go get him."

"Give him some more time. He's got to be thinking he's in love by now."

"I'm sure he is. That's why we need to go in there and get him."

Wesley groaned, then climbed out of the car with me. We made our way up to the porch again and pounded on the door. It took Dolores a lot longer to answer this time. Wesley started filming with his cellphone again.

She opened the door with a dazed look on her face, like she'd been up to no good, and John was lying half naked on the couch in her living room. She leaned into me and reached for my sunglasses. I swatted her hand away.

"Ow!" She sneered at me. "You don't have to be mean about it."

"You don't have to be grabby."

John saw me slap her hand and jumped up from the couch. "Don't hit her! What's wrong with you?"

"We're here to take you back home."

"I'm not ready to go." John folded his arms over his chest and sat back down on the couch.

Dolores grabbed my hand and pulled me in a few inches toward her. "Why don't you come in, Ray? It'll be just like old times. Remember all the fun we had?"

"How can I forget?"

I nudged her to the side and yelled in at John, "Let's get going."

"John," Wesley yelled, "get your ass up. We're leaving."

Dolores ran her fingers across my cheek then up into my hair. I cringed. "No sense in flirting with me. I'm happily married."

Dolores giggled. "What does that have anything to do with it? I know how to keep a secret."

John groaned and stood up. He slipped on his clothes and glanced around the room. "I'm thirsty."

"You all can come in for drinks. I have plenty."

"No, thanks." Wesley eyed John. "We have beer in the car."

"I want water," John moaned.

"You can wait till we get home."

Dolores grinned. "I think he should stay the night. We were just starting to get to know each other."

"I want to stay all night." John walked up behind Dolores. "I've got everything I need here. Why do I got to leave?"

"You can't stay. Too much of a good thing isn't healthy for a man like you."

John wrapped his arms around Dolores and pulled her in tighter next to him.

Wesley filmed the whole thing and laughed. "You two get close now."

John put his face up to her cheek and kissed her several times. "Did you get that?"

"Yep."

I reached in and pulled John away from Dolores. His arm slipped away, but he tugged back. I thought we might be in for a fight to get him out of there, but Wesley joined in and we got him outside before things got ugly. Same thing happened to me when I was in that situation. Except back then, Wesley had to bring a few of his friends to pry me away from her. Thank God he did.

"I don't want to go," John said. "Dolores promised to show me her garden in the backyard."

"I'm sure she did."

"He can stay the night." Dolores reached for John's hand, but I stood in the way.

"I'm staying the night." John pushed past me to go back inside.

Wesley stopped the video then and grabbed John's upper arm. "I can't do that to you, Johnny boy."

"Why not?"

Wesley shook his head. "You'd regret it."

"Why would I regret it? I'm the happiest I've ever been in my life. You were right. She *is* the girl of my dreams."

"Oh, you're so sweet." Dolores swatted her hand toward John.

"You just wait," Wesley said.

"For what?"

"You'll see."

John smirked. "Tell me. Does she turn into a frog in the morning?"

"Nope. No frog."

John lurched forward back into her house.

Dolores blocked me and Wesley from grabbing him again. "He wants to stay the night."

Wesley laughed louder, but didn't chase John past the threshold. "Okay, birthday boy, if that's what you want to do."

"That's what I want to do," John repeated.

"Have it your way, smarty pants. I'm telling you right now you're making a mistake, but I'll do what you want, and I don't want to hear you bitching at me tomorrow either on the way home. Got it?"

"Why would I bitch about anything?"

"Oh, you will. But seeing as though it's your birthday and I want you to have a real nice time, I'll let you enjoy the evening—both of you."

"You're so sweet." Dolores's grin widened, and she ran her hands down the front of Wesley's shirt.

"Get your hands off me." Wesley stepped back.

John walked over and sat on her couch. "You can come over here and do that to me."

Wesley shivered. "Yeah, why don't you do that to him. It's his birthday after all, right?"

"I'm the birthday boy," John said. "Do you have any more presents for me?"

Dolores giggled and ran over to John as he sprawled out on her couch. "I got lots of big presents for you tonight."

My stomach churned, and I cringed. "Yeah, just live it up, John. Have the time of your life."

"Thanks, guys, I will."

We went back to the car, and it was almost 2 in the morning before we got home. Wesley called me around noon the next day saying he hadn't heard from John yet so we drove over there to take him home.

We parked in the same spot as the night before and, despite being the middle of the day, the forest was dark as ever.

We put on our sunglasses again and knocked on the door. Dolores opened it and John was standing in his pajamas behind her. His hair was a mess, but he smiled.

"Did you just get up?" I asked.

"I didn't get much sleep last night."

Wesley laughed. "Who's pajamas are those?"

John look down at his clothes. "Dolores got them for me."

"Where did she get them?"

"I always have an extra pair in case of emergencies." Dolores glared at Wesley.

"You're wearing someone else's clothes, Johnny."

John shrugged. "Doesn't matter."

Dolores snuggled up next to him.

I chuckled and nudged Wesley. "He looks so happy."

"He does." Wesley nodded. "Just remember this time, John. Enjoy the moment."

John scowled. "You're making it sound like I'm not ever coming back here again. Dolores said I can come back any time, right?" He looked into her eyes.

She snuggled in closer to him. "You can come back any time you want. You want to marry me? Okay."

John stuck out his chest. "It doesn't get better than this, guys. I'm in love."

Wesley stepped toward John, but stopped short of entering the house. "John, we just need you to come back home now. You can return again sometime if you really want."

John kissed Dolores's forehead. "Did you hear what she just said? She said she'd marry me. The girl of my dreams wants to marry me. I'm the happiest guy alive."

"Let's just get you back to the house, lover boy, and let you think things over."

"I don't need to think anything over. Dolores loves me and that's all that matters."

"You don't understand."

"Understand what? What's the problem? I'm happy. Why do you guys want to mess with me?"

"You'll understand better when we get home."

"Wesley, don't spoil our fun." Dolores cuddled in John's arms.

Wesley nodded. "Okay, John. I'll make a deal with you. You come back to the car for thirty minutes with us and after that if you feel you want to go back in the house with Dolores, then fine with me. All I need is thirty minutes to talk with you alone."

John sighed. "I'm not changing out of my pajamas."

"You can leave your jammies on. Let's go talk." Wesley gestured for John to follow us.

"Fine." John put on some brown slippers next to the door and walked outside with us. "I'll be back, Dolores. I need to straighten this man out, seeing as though he insists on ruining our day. Just thirty minutes."

"I'll be here waiting for you." She blew him a kiss. "Just remember that I love you."

"I love you too," John said.

Wesley stood on one side of John and I stood on the other side. I kept my hands up next to his arm in case he spun around and tried to escape back to her. He glanced back several times on the way to the car, waving and throwing kisses before we pushed him into the backseat. Wesley climbed in next to him and I locked the doors.

We took off our sunglasses as Wesley fiddled with his cellphone.

John blurted out, "Wowsy yowsy! She's got it all. I can't

believe my luck. This is the best birthday ever. I'm glad you guys got it on video so I can look back and remember this day when we get old. You guys missed your chance with her and now I'm going to marry that girl."

Wesley laughed. "You want to marry Dolores? That's the funniest damn thing I've ever heard."

"What's so funny? Didn't you hear what she said? She'd marry me."

"Nobody will marry Dolores."

"Why the hell not? She already said she would. Who's going to stop me?"

John sneered and brought up his fists.

"Easy, John. No one's trying to start a fight."

Wesley turned around his cellphone's screen so John could see it. "Okay, okay. I got to show you something before you get all riled up."

"See what? You better not have made some awful video of us to post on YouTube. I won't stand for you guys disrespecting Dolores."

"Nobody's disrespecting her. Just watch the video."

Wesley played the video and John watched it expressionless for the longest time. I peeked around and watched it with him. Confusion spread over John's face after Dolores appeared in the doorway.

"Who's that? What did you do to Dolores? This isn't funny."

"That's the girl of your dreams."

"What did you do to her? You put some joke video filter on her face, didn't you? Some special effects from one of those apps that messes up how people look."

"No man. That's how she looks in real life."

"Bullshit. That's not her. Dolores is a beautiful twenty something. You made her look like she's ninety-five years old. That's just mean."

"She might be ninety-five, or maybe even older than that. Dolores is a witch. I just wanted you to have a fun time and there's no shame in that. We did the same thing when we were young. We got taken in just like you did. You had fun though, didn't you? You had the time of your life?"

John just stared with his mouth hanging open.

"You had fun. That's great and you deserve it. You're my favorite cousin, John, so I hope you had a wonderful birthday. Dolores puts a trance on anyone who sees her and whatever you want her to look like, that's what she looks like. No shame in what you've done. I just wanted you to have a great birthday."

John continued to stare and shook his head. "No, that's not her. That woman's uglier than a rock."

Wesley nodded. "Yep. She tricked you and me and Ray, and anyone else who looks at her. She would've tricked us last night too if we weren't looking at her through these sunglasses. Something about polarized sunglasses messes up her trance. Doesn't work when they're on."

He gazed at me and then back to Wesley. He furled his brows. "You mean, she's really not pretty? She really looks like that old hag?"

"She's not bad or anything—at least, I don't *think* so. Maybe if she were sixty years younger, we might work something out, but I'm afraid that's the way things are. I tried to get you out of there last night before she dragged you deeper into her spell, but you didn't listen. I made the video so you would believe me and we could all have a little laugh. You had a good time, right?"

"We've been through it too, John. It's just a little prank. Hope you're not mad."

John slowly shook his head. "No. I'm not mad. Give me those sunglasses."

"What for?"

"I have to see it for myself."

Wesley nodded. "We did the same thing. We didn't believe it either, at first."

I handed John my pair of sunglasses and he slipped them on.

"I'll be right back," he said, climbing out of the backseat.

"Don't take them off," Wesley said.

He didn't answer. He slammed the door and hurried back to Dolores's front porch. She stood in the doorway as he walked up to her.

"Maybe we should go over there," Wesley suggested.

"Do you think he might try to hurt her?"

"He might. He's a good kid, but I think he's pissed."

We stepped out of the car and walked toward the house.

I avoided looking at Dolores, forcing myself to only see her from the corner of my eye. John ran his hand along the side of Dolores's face and they talked for a moment. He pulled her inside the house, then emerged a few minutes later still in his pajamas. He took off the sunglasses and tossed them out toward us.

"You guys go home." John gestured for us to leave.

We stopped. "Are you sure?"

"Yeah, I'm staying here. I'll call you later."

I picked up the sunglasses and the front door slammed shut.

"Well, that ain't what I expected." Wesley's eyes widened. "Should we go in there and drag him out?"

"What for? Let him have his fun."

Wesley laughed most of the way back home.

CASSETTE

Blair hovered over Jake as he slipped the black cassette tape into the player.

"What are you doing?" she asked.

"What does it look like I'm doing?"

"Wasting time listening to a bunch of cruddy old cassette tapes. You might as well just throw those things out."

"That's your solution to everything, isn't it? Just throw it out."

"You're so defensive, Jake. I'm your wife, remember?"

"You always remind me." Jake rewound the tape. "These are valuable. Some of the last items from my childhood."

Blair dug into Jake's tote of childhood possessions and pulled out an old leather gun holster. She held it up with two fingers as if it were a piece of rotting flesh. "What's this thing?"

Jake glanced at it. "Something I used to play with."

"You wanted to be a cowboy?"

"Anything wrong with that?"

"I guess not." She dropped it back into the tote. "Seems kind of silly, considering you grew up in New York City."

"I just wanted to get out of there and have an adventure. I was a kid."

"Can't hang on to the past forever." Blair grunted and left the room.

After the bedroom door clicked shut, Jake hit play on the tape deck. His cousin Logan's voice blared out the name of their imaginary radio show, the "Jake and Logan Mystery Hour," as if they were famous entertainers. Without a pause, they jumped into their first skit. Jake's youthful voice brought a smile to his face. Even back when he was eleven years old he knew he wanted to entertain people.

It surprised him that any of his old cassette tapes had survived for so many years. Most of his childhood possessions had gotten thrown out by his minimalist parents after he'd left home for college, and he'd adopted the same habit of clearing clutter on a regular basis. Only one plastic tote left.

He grinned as he listened to the tape. Two decades had passed since he and his cousin had filled up several tapes with goofy, ranting sketches. Most of their antics made no sense now, but back then it had been magical. They recorded some of the best times of his life during those carefree summer days. Listening to his childish voice now was almost surreal. Familiar, yet like listening to a complete stranger.

The audio played and transported Jake back to that summer afternoon.

Logan: "Here's the train, Jake, it's coming over the mountain. Are you watching?"

Jake: "Aaah, lookout!"

Logan: "Get out of my way, you moron."

Jake: "Turn!"

Logan: "I am turning. I can't stop! All the way up the mountain, then down the other side. Aaah, I can't stop! I'm going to crash!" (crash and explosion sounds)

Jake: "All fourteen passengers are presumed dead after smashing through the side of a building at the base of the railway. Seven additional bystanders were killed in the collision."

Logan: "Someone call an ambulance! I think they're dead!"

Jake furrowed his brow. That was strange. He and Logan had said a lot of crazy things in the tape recordings—that's just how eleven-year-olds talked back then—but Jake didn't remember saying anything so grown-up and morbid.

The urge to call his cousin popped into his mind, to ask him about what they'd recorded, but that time had passed. Logan was gone. Dead from a car accident a few days earlier. Jake hadn't even bothered to tell Blair about his loss. She wouldn't care, anyway. That's how their relationship had developed the last couple of years. He'd gotten used to it.

Jake glanced at the digital clock on his desk. 6:36pm. The funeral would be over by then and his cousin was six feet under. He would have been at the funeral, but he'd had too many other things to take care of—one of them, to prepare for Blair's birthday party.

The doorbell rang and Jake stopped the tape. He went out into the living room just as his wife answered the door.

Victor Thompson and Steve Barlow had arrived early. Two guys always looking for a good time. Blair greeted them with her usual over-enthusiasm.

Victor spotted Jake standing behind Blair and formed one of his usual phony smiles—a smirk—then handed Blair a bottle of champagne with a bow around the neck.

"Happy Birthday!" Victor switched to a more genuine smile when Blair gave him a hug.

She wrapped her arms around him and held him a little too long.

Jake rolled his eyes and approached Victor when Blair took the champagne to the kitchen.

"Are we going to have a good time, or what?" Victor stepped inside and took off his shoes.

"I hope so," Jake said.

"You hope so? You don't sound too sure."

Jake shrugged.

Steve Barlow walked around Victor and headed straight to the living room. He switched on the TV and dropped into the couch. "You guys need to get a bigger television. 40 inches doesn't cut it anymore."

"Sorry, Steve," Blair said from the kitchen, "I know you like your big screens."

"Just for the games."

"Jake insists we don't need a bigger one."

"Blame it on me." Jake turned to Victor and shook his hand. Cold and clammy. "Enjoy the party, Victor."

"I intend to." Victor nudged past him to get to Blair, who was digging out food and beer from the fridge. He rattled off a crude joke and Blair broke out laughing. She was always laughing at his stupid jokes. Nobody else would listen to them, and they were *stupid* jokes. Not even something a child would think was funny. Not a single intelligent bone in Victor's body.

A short while later, the Crane twins arrived, Alivia and Alice. Brazilian girls who Blair had met while getting her Masters Degree in Communication Studies at the University of Minnesota. They presented her with a small, pink gift bag. Blair opened it right away. An assortment of body lotions. Blair raved about the gift, set it on the counter, then set them up with drinks.

Another couple arrived an hour later. Danny and Amy. Everyone was single, except Jake and Blair.

Jake hovered between them, striking up brief conversations to hear what they'd done since their last party. He downed two beers, watching the interactions with feigned interest. They were Blair's friends. He was the outsider, even after three years of marriage.

Victor moved in and flirted with Blair again. Same maneuver every party. He slinked in toward her during their conversation and tapped the side of her stomach. Tap, tap, tap. She giggled, then talked a little louder. Not too obvious, but Jake had noticed Mr. Slick months earlier.

It made no difference anyway. Jake and Blair had long since gotten past the jealous stage in their marriage. She could do whatever she wanted with that unfunny slime ball.

Jake helped himself to another beer in the refrigerator while Victor poured Blair a glass of the champagne he'd brought for her.

So smooth, Victor.

Despite the abundance of alcohol in their house, Danny and Amy brought a bottle of wine, and Steve Barlow brought a bottle of Captain Morgan rum, but he would consume the gift soon enough.

The Crane twins wore tight skirts, Alice in blue and Alivia in purple, as if they were in for a night on the town. They wiggled and danced in place at the slightest sound of music. Danny and Amy talked with them at the edge of the living room until Steve broke away from the TV and lumbered over to join their group. He threw his arms around both twins and juggled his attention between them as they laughed. Steve's jokes were actually funny.

Jake crossed into the kitchen and grabbed a beer before sitting down in his usual spot on the couch in front of the TV. Alivia caught his gaze and broke away from the others. She walked over and sat down next to him. Jake breathed in her rosy scent and smiled.

She leaned in close, rubbing her knee against his leg, and talked about the joys of her new job in marketing, but he had little interest in listening to stories about anybody's job. He only wanted to forget about life's problems, his cousin's funeral, and just get drunk. Any talk of work brought his mind back to his own job—graphic design—and all the headaches waiting for him on Monday morning.

Jake glanced back toward the kitchen. Victor's voice boomed across the room. The life of the party, the driving force behind their frequent get-togethers. Victor rattled on about the successes of his gaming company, and all the celebrities he'd met while recording their voice-over for various characters. Elijah Wood, Mark Hamill, Ellen Page, and Samuel L. Jackson.

Jake had listened to all the stories several times now, but Blair still insisted on hearing them all again. She hung on Victor's every word.

Victor vented another poor joke, followed by Blair's laughter. Jake glanced back at them just as she touched Victor's arm.

"Oh, you should take your jokes to the comedy club," Blair said. "I love the stories you tell. You could be a standup comedian."

So much bullshit. Why did she keep encouraging him to tell those same stories over and over? Jake would need to have a long conversation with Blair in the morning.

"Are you and Blair planning anything special for your anniversary?"

Jake paused and shrugged. He'd forgotten all about it. Only four days away. "She has to work."

"Have you thought about taking a trip to Brazil? It's so beautiful."

"Maybe someday. Blair doesn't get much time off."

"I travel back there every year to visit some family. I could meet you down there and take you to the best places away from all the tourists."

Victor's voice rose and fell in the background.

Alivia's brown eyes calmed him. "That sounds good."

Steve flipped through the TV channels, pausing on a

breaking news story. "... The cable used to tow the tourist trolley to the top of Corcovado mountain in Rio de Janeiro broke free, sending it hurling to the bottom at over 90mph. All fourteen passengers are presumed dead after smashing through the side of a building at the base of the railway. Seven additional bystanders were killed in the collision."

Alivia gasped. "Oh God!"

Jake paused. The news stunned him. Not just the news, but the exact words the announcer had used.

All fourteen passengers are presumed dead after smashing through the side of a building at the base of the railway. Seven additional bystanders were killed in the collision.

He'd heard those words somewhere before.

"So horrible!" Alivia gazed at him. "Are you okay?"

Jake glanced around the room. "That's weird. I think I'm having deja vu."

Alivia's brow furrowed. "Really?"

Jake nodded. "What that news guy just said—I've heard it before."

Alivia nudged him. "Too much beer."

"Not this time. Something's different. It feels strange, like everything's a dream. Maybe I'm going nuts."

"You got that right," Blair said from the kitchen.

Jake sneered. "Don't be a smartass, Blair. Just drink your champagne."

Alivia touched his hand. "My mom said that when someone has deja vu, they're remembering a dream they had. Or maybe you're repeating a conversation you had in a previous life."

Alice jumped in and corrected her. "Reincarnation is bullshit, Alivia."

"Well, *I* believe it. Whatever it is, it's strange."

The deja vu faded as Jake downed the rest of his beer. "I know I've heard that line before."

"Maybe you're psychic." Alivia squinted as she gazed into his eyes.

Jake shrugged.

"What am I thinking?" The corners of her mouth rose as she leaned closer.

"Naughty things, I'm sure."

Alivia slapped his arm, but didn't pull away. "I was thinking you should get me another drink."

"Jake," Blair said from the kitchen. "Don't be flirting with the twins."

Alice and Alivia laughed.

"It's okay," Alivia said. "We've gotten used to Jake by now. He's harmless."

Jake glanced back at Blair. Victor continued with his story and put his hand on her arm.

Jake grunted. They would need to talk in the morning.

The TV news reporter's strange sentence ran through his mind again. He'd heard that line before. Not just deja vu or remembering it in a dream, but from somewhere else.

The tape. He'd heard those same words on the cassette tape. His own eleven-year-old self had said those exact same phrases twenty years earlier, but how was that possible? Just a circumstance? Why would an eleven-year-old kid say something like that? But maybe he remembered it wrong. He couldn't get it out of his mind. He had to go back to the stereo and listen to it again. The beer wasn't screwing with him—it was on the cassette tape for sure, and he'd prove it.

Jake repeated the words of the newscaster over and over in his mind as he got up and went into his office.

All fourteen passengers are presumed dead after smashing through the side of a building at the base of the railway. Seven additional bystanders were killed in the collision.

He closed the door and sat in front of the stereo system.

He rewound the cassette, skipping back, then a little forward to find the exact moment he'd said the line.

Jake: "I'm almost done."

Logan: "Here's the train, Jake, it's coming over the mountain. Are you watching?"

Jake: "Aaah, lookout!"

Logan: "Get out of my way, you moron."

Jake: "Turn!"

Logan: "I am turning. I can't stop! All the way up the mountain, then down the other side. Aaah, I can't stop! I'm going to crash!"

Jake: "Who knows what a crazy person might do with a weapon like that?"

Logan: "Put the gun down, you psychopath!

Jake: (sound of gunshot) "Aaah! You shot me!"

Logan: "Someone call an ambulance! I think he's dead!"

Jake: (death noises) "How could you do such a thing?" (body collapsing)

Not the same line. Not even close. He'd remembered it wrong. Alivia was right, it must be the beer.

The new conversation made even less sense than the one he'd originally heard. The words streamed through his thoughts again and again. Such a strange thing to say for an eleven-year-old. But he'd said and done so many stupid things back then. Anything was possible for an imaginative child.

The sense of deja vu flooded back to him. What was going on? Something straight from a Hitchcock movie. In the morning, he would listen to the tape again, and maybe then it would all make sense.

Jake shut off the stereo system and walked out of his office.

Blair cut him off on the way to the living room. "Where were you?"

"I had to take care of something."

"You were gone for thirty minutes."

"Was I?" Jake looked at the time on his cellphone. "It seemed like just a few minutes."

"Did you take a nap? Don't crash yet. It's my birthday, remember? And we have friends over."

"I wasn't asleep." Jake pressed his palm to his forehead. "I feel weird."

Blair eyed him with concern for a moment, then sneered at him and sniffed his shirt. "Did you smoke a little weed while you were in your office? Are you high?"

"Not this time. I feel kind of... out of it, like things aren't real."

"Put down the beer." Blair grabbed at his beer, but he pulled back.

"It's not the beer."

"Did you guzzle some shots of Jack when I wasn't looking? Are you drunk already?"

"I'm not drunk at all. Well, not yet."

"Just don't embarrass me again, okay? Drink some water for a change."

Blair gazed into his eyes, then went back to Victor Thompson's side. Within seconds they were laughing it up. Blair whispered something to Victor, then he glared back at Jake as if he'd done something wrong.

Jake lumbered into the living room and returned to his spot on the couch next to Alivia.

"Do you feel better?" she asked.

"A little."

"Maybe you should go lie down."

"I'm okay." He finished another beer and stared at the television. Someone had turned the channel to a football game. Steve hoarded the remote next to Amy and sat fixated on the screen.

Danny emerged from the bathroom waving a silver pistol over his head. "Look what I found."

Jake's breath stopped at the sight of his antique .45 Colt revolver in Danny's hand. How the hell had he found it? It was safely stowed away in Jake's office closet.

"Put that down!" Alivia put up her hands.

Jake stood and approached Danny. "What are you doing? Are you drunk?"

"No, but you are."

"I'm not."

"You are definitely drunk, Jake. I can see the future. I predict you'll be curled up on the floor in a corner by the end of the night."

Jake reached for his revolver. "How did you get that? Were you snooping in my office?"

"So, it's yours then?"

"Yeah, it's mine. Give it here."

"I wasn't in your office, Jake. I found it in the bathroom next to the sink. Do you always keep your guns lying around like this?"

"Oh no. That's my fault," Blair said. "I left it there by accident. Jake left it out on the coffee table this afternoon after he spent *way* too much time cleaning it. I meant to put it back in his office, but I forgot. Sorry about that. I must have gotten distracted and left it in the bathroom. I hope it's not loaded."

"I never leave it loaded," Jake said.

Danny stood several inches higher than Jake and used it to his advantage to keep the revolver out of Jake's hands. "Is it loaded, Jake? Did you leave a loaded gun out on the coffee table?"

"I don't leave loaded guns lying around. Give it back." Jake lost his smile. "I'm not goofing around."

"You're not?" Danny chuckled and examined the pistol. "This thing's old."

"It's a .45 Colt Single Action Army Revolver. The gun that won the west."

Danny spun it around his trigger finger twice and backed away as Jake reached for it. "Is it a real Wild West gun?"

"What do you think?"

Danny nodded. "I like it. Maybe a cowboy killed some outlaws with this thing. Where did you get it?"

"I inherited it."

"So maybe your descendants killed some people with this."

"Maybe."

"Cool." Danny pointed the gun at Jake's face with a wide grin. The barrel's tip wavered only inches from Jake's forehead when Danny pulled the trigger.

Click.

"What the hell?" Jake grabbed the barrel and yanked it away. "You better knock that shit off."

"You're right. It wasn't loaded." Danny laughed. "Don't worry, I checked it before I came out."

"You're a fucking psychopath."

"Don't get all testy. I wouldn't have pranked you unless I knew it was empty. You think I would point a loaded gun at you without checking it first?"

"Yeah."

"I wouldn't. I'm not that stupid. Don't get all severe on me now. It's just a joke, okay? We're having a great time for Blair's party, so chill out."

Jake's face warmed. "I'm chilled out just fine, but you better not point that gun at me again or I'll beat your ass with it."

Danny raised his eyebrows. "Beat your ass. What a drunk thing to say."

"Dickhead."

Danny walked past Jake, laughing on his way to the living

room. "You should probably lock that gun away, Blair. A dangerous person might get his hands on it. Who knows what a crazy person might do with a weapon like that? Do you agree?"

Those words. Deja vu rushed in again.

Who knows what a crazy person might do with a weapon like that?

The cassette tape. A chill passed up his spine. He'd said those same words on the tape.

"What's wrong, Jake?" Danny asked him. "You look like you just shit your pants."

Everyone laughed, except Alivia and Alice.

He tried to smile. "I think I'm having deja vu again."

Danny whistled an eerie melody. "Maybe you're dreaming. This is all an illusion, Jake," he said in a hypnotic voice. "Soon you'll wake up and discover yourself sitting on a tropical beach."

They laughed again.

Alivia walked over and pressed her palm on his forehead. Her warm hand comforted him for a moment. She stared into his eyes. "You don't have a fever. But I think you should lie down for five minutes. Your face is pale."

"I'm okay."

"Jake, stop flirting with Alivia."

"He's not flirting with me, Blair," Alivia said. "I told him to go lay down."

Blair sneered at him. "I suppose."

Who knows what a crazy person might do with a weapon like that?

Jake hurried back to his office clutching the revolver and closed the door. He rewound the tape again and played it back near the start of the section he'd listened to earlier. He needed to hear those words again, just to make sure he wasn't going crazy.

Logan: "Hurry up, Jake."

Jake: "I'm almost done."

Logan: "Here's the train, Jake, it's coming over the mountain. Are you watching?"

Jake: "Aaah, lookout!"

Logan: "Get out of my way, you moron."

Jake: "Turn!"

Logan: "I am turning. I can't stop! All the way up the mountain, then down the other side. Aaah, I can't stop! I'm going to crash!"

Jake: "Don't do anything stupid, stupid."

Logan: "Put the gun down, you psychopath!"

Jake: (sound of gunshot) "Aaah! You shot me!"

Logan: "Someone call an ambulance! I think he's dead!"

Jake: (death noises) "How could you do such a thing?"

Logan: "I shoot bad guys. That's what I do."

Jake switched off the cassette player. Different words now. His stomach churned and he wiped his damp forehead. If the previous version of the lines had come true, then someone was about to get shot. No, that couldn't be right.

Jake glanced over at the pistol on his desk. No need to panic. He had the only gun, and if the words came true, someone might say them on a TV show just like what had happened with the trolley crash on the news.

Someone call an ambulance! I think he's dead!

Jake slid the pistol into the bottom drawer of his desk. As long as it remained in there, nobody would get shot in his house. Everything would be fine. The strange sense of deja vu didn't mean that the lines had to happen in actual life.

He lumbered out to the living room and forced a smile.

"Are you okay?" Steve asked him from the couch. "Your face is white like you just saw a ghost."

"Nobody has a gun on them, right?"

Everyone stared back at him with blank expressions.

"Why?" Alice asked.

Danny turned away from his girlfriend Amy and took a step forward. "You lookin' to pick a gunfight? I'm ready for ya." He scowled as he held the TV remote at his waist like a gun in a holster.

Jake shook his head. "I'm serious."

"I am too. Now *draw*!"

"I've got this one, Jake," Steve jumped up from the couch, also with a pretend gun at his side, and faced Danny. "Don't do anything stupid, stupid."

Danny sneered at Steve. "Put the gun down, you psychopath!"

Steve drew his imaginary pistol and fired.

"Aaah!" Danny recoiled as if someone had shot him in the chest. "You shot me!" He tumbled back onto the couch and faked his death.

Alice jumped in beside him and raised his limp arm before dropping it again. "Someone call an ambulance! I think he's dead!"

Danny choked and gasped for air. He sprang back to life and reached out his hand toward Steve. "How could you do such a thing?"

Steve blew smoke off the tip of his imaginary pistol. "I shoot bad guys. That's what I do."

Everyone laughed.

Jake's mind reeled. The exact words from the tape. At least nobody had gotten hurt.

"Nobody's packing heat at Blair's birthday party." Victor held up his hands. "Want to frisk me?"

Blair pushed Victor's hands down. "Don't mind Jake. He's drunk."

"Should we go home and get our weapons, Jake?" Danny asked. "Something going down soon?"

"No, I... never mind. I'm just a little tired."

The football game blared on the TV as Jake walked to the

kitchen. Victor and Blair veered out of his way as he poured himself a glass of water.

"What's this all about?" Victor asked. "You worried we might start something? We're all friends here, right?"

"Yes," Jake said, "nothing like that. I'm just having that deja vu again."

"Go lay down then." Blair turned away from him.

He walked back toward his bedroom with his head throbbing, then stopped. What would the tape say now? He paused and stared at his office door a few feet down the hall. Everything on the tape had come true, although strangely. Maybe now he'd hear the playful voices he and his cousin had truly spoken twenty years earlier.

He turned into his office and closed the door. Blair wouldn't bother him now. He wouldn't be able to calm his mind until he knew everything was back to normal.

He sat down and rewound the tape. Hitting play, his body tensed.

Logan: "Let's go to my place."

Jake: "He's right outside. He'll see us leave."

Logan: "He won't see anything. He's drunk. He'll pass out on the floor again."

Jake: "It is my special day, but not yet."

Logan: "We'll wait until he's asleep."

Jake: "You two look like outlaws to me. Get ready to draw."

Logan: "Don't point that thing at us, you psychopath!"

Jake: "I'm the new sheriff in these parts. You two varmints are under arrest."

Logan: "Stop goofing around. That thing better not be loaded."

Jake: "Put that away. Not—"

Logan: (sound of gunshot) (scream) "Oh, my God!"

Jake: (sound of gunshot) "Shit!"

Logan: (death noises)

Jake: "What the hell?"

Logan: "What happened? You shot them!"
Jake: "I... He said it wasn't loaded."
Logan: "Call an ambulance!"
Jake: "I didn't mean to."
Logan: "What were you thinking?"
Jake: "We have to stop the bleeding."
Logan: "Check their pulse."
Jake: (crying) "It's too late. They're dead."

Jake stopped the tape. His eyes widened and his jaw dropped open. What had just happened? Not only had the words on the tape changed but no child could have imagined such a horrific scene during an afternoon playtime. Despite the strangeness of the dialogue, the cowboy references were undeniable.

Jake stared at the pistol on his desk beside him. How could something so specific and horrible happen in the future? His pistol wasn't even loaded.

He sipped his water and stared at the handwritten names across the front of the cassette tape in the player. Jake and Logan's Mystery Hour.

He couldn't have said any of those lines as an eleven-year-old. He'd said many strange things back then, but those words had never come out of his mouth. Yet there they were on the tape. And if the previous versions of the lines proved anything, they would come true.

But how could they come true? He never loaded his pistol in the house. Ever.

The words of his wife came back to him. Can't hang on to the past forever.

But he loved her. Did he?

He'd rid himself of the mementos from their early romance and marriage. Nothing in his office to remind him of her. And they'd long given up on date nights or talking about having a child.

Jake picked up the pistol and turned it over in his hands. Clean and ready to go. There would be witnesses and no chance of anyone to suspect him.

He set the pistol down again and dug through the bottom drawer of his desk. A box of rounds sat in the corner. He opened the box and picked out six. The metal cooled his palm. He only needed two if the recording was right. No, better to have six for the inevitable investigation. He placed the six rounds end-up on his desk and closed the drawer.

A faint grin stretched out from the corners of his mouth. Was he evil? *He* wasn't doing anything wrong, technically, except allowing fate to take its course. Maybe nothing would happen anyway. No chance to know for sure if the tape's conversation would come true, but the others had. And this one was so *specific*. All too perfect. How could he pass it up?

Jake loaded the rounds into the revolver's chambers and snapped the cylinder shut.

He wouldn't need to do anything. Just set the pistol on the desk like before and let fate do its thing. Everything would take care of itself.

Someone knocked on the door. Jake shuddered. Alivia opened it and peeked in at him. "Are you okay?"

He got up from his desk and stepped to her. "Sure, I'm fine."

"Would you like to get some fresh air?"

A devious grin passed over her face. His heart beat faster. He would love to see that grin every day for the rest of his life.

Jake nodded. "Let's go."

She grabbed his arm and glanced back at his desk. "Shouldn't you put your gun away?"

"No, nobody comes in here."

"We can go out the back."

He paused and gazed into her eyes. "I'm glad I have you in my life, Alivia."

Her eyes widened as she beamed. "I feel the same way." She pressed her head against his shoulder.

She led Jake out through the living room toward the back door. Neither Blair nor Victor noticed. Alice and Steve were snuggling closer on the couch in the living room. Amy stood next to Danny near the kitchen table.

Danny guzzled his beer and pretended to pull a pistol from his imaginary holster. "Gotcha. Where are you guys off to?"

"Get some air." Jake feigned nausea. The butterflies in his stomach multiplied with the excitement building in his mind.

"You look a little better now."

Jake shrugged. "I think I'll feel better tomorrow."

As he headed out the door with Alivia at his side, he glanced back to Blair and Victor. One of his hands moved across her waist.

Can't hang onto the past forever.

Jake and Alivia moved out into the cool night air.

She snuggled in closer to him and stared up at the night sky. "I'd like to travel the world someday. Have you ever thought about doing that?"

"I love adventures." Jake walked until he heard the gunshots and the screams. He didn't even flinch as Alivia turned back in confusion toward the house.

"What was that?" She stared at him with wide eyes.

Jake covered his mouth to hide his wide grin. "I don't know. Let's go see."

MORE FRIGHTFUL FUN!

Get Book 4 now on Amazon.com!

Dreadful Dark Tales of Horror Book 4

books2read.com/DreadfulDark-Book04

Shocking stories with a toxic twist...

Two young men are lured into the forest by a naked woman and discover she's not wholly what she seems to be. A widower rids himself of his wife's stuffed Pomeranian she left behind to protect him, but discovers the deceased dog takes his job seriously. A motel guest books the last room in town, but discovers a previous tenant might not have checked out.

More novels and stories coming soon!
You can sign up to be notified of new releases
and pre-releases
— PLUS get a **FREE** short story at my website!

https://books2read.com/StoneHill-BookOfCrane

www.deanrasmussen.com

★★★★★
Please review my book!

If you liked this book and have a moment to spare, I would greatly appreciate a short review on the page where you bought it. Your help in spreading the word is *immensely* appreciated and reviews make a huge difference in helping new readers find my novels.

All FREE on Kindle Unlimited:

Hanging House: An Emmie Rose Haunted Mystery Book 1
Caine House: An Emmie Rose Haunted Mystery Book 2
Hyde House: An Emmie Rose Haunted Mystery Book 3

Dreadful Dark Tales of Horror Book 1
Dreadful Dark Tales of Horror Book 2
Dreadful Dark Tales of Horror Book 3
Dreadful Dark Tales of Horror Book 4
Dreadful Dark Tales of Horror Book 5
Dreadful Dark Tales of Horror Book 6
Dreadful Dark Tales of Horror Box Set Books 1 - 3

Stone Hill: Shadows Rising (Book 1)
Stone Hill: Phantoms Reborn (Book 2)
Stone Hill: Leviathan Wakes (Book 3)

ABOUT THE AUTHOR

Dean Rasmussen grew up in a small Minnesota town and began writing stories at the age of ten, driven by his fascination with the Star Wars hero's journey. He continued writing short stories and attempted a few novels through his early twenties until he stopped to focus on his computer animation ambitions. He studied English at a Minnesota college during that time.

He learned the art of computer animation and went on to work on twenty feature films, a television show, and a AAA video game as a visual effects artist over thirteen years.

Dean currently teaches animation for visual effects in Orlando, Florida. Inspired by his favorite authors, Stephen King, Ray Bradbury, and H. P. Lovecraft, Dean began writing novels and short stories again in 2018 to thrill and delight a new generation of horror fans.